Please return/renew this item by the
last date shown to avoid a charge.
Books may also be renewed by phone
and Internet. May not be renewed if
required by another reader.

www.libraries.barnet.gov.uk

LONDON BOROUGH

you knew, or could rely on'   Sophie Elmhirst, *New Statesman*

'A wonderful collection: entertaining, profound and gently
powerful. It confirms Englander's stature as a serious comic
voice'   Alison Kelly, *TLS*

'Eng   ely light
touc

'There is high literary talent here . . . enjoy Englander's mastery of the simplest, and hardest, form of writing – storytelling'
Herald

'Englander's prose is simply beautiful, whether in dialogue or third-person; precise and poised, able to introduce the grit of reality while preserving the balance of the sentence' *Scotsman*

'Takes vignettes from Jewish life and explores them with a humane understanding of the human condition in all its painful absurdity, lending them a universal significance . . . a small masterpiece of tragic restraint' *Daily Mail*

'Mr Englander knows where to hold back, a particular gift when writing about and around the martyr of his title, the locked up and locked in . . . terrific collection'
International Herald Tribune

'It requires great control and confidence to operate with any consistency at the point where humour grates so excruciatingly against calamity. In the best of this collection, Englander proves he has both' Tim Martin, *Daily Telegraph*

'Will leave you open-mouthed' *Jewish Chronicle*

'Glorious . . . Like all genuinely comic writers, he is profoundly serious – and moral. Nevertheless, his dialogue-rich stories move with a zing' *Financial Times*

'Nathan Englander is a master of the short story and one of the great voices of our time. *What We Talk About When We Talk About Anne Frank* showcases Englander's comic genius and lacerating vision of human nature as never before, in stories that are audacious, expertly crafted, and often unforgettably beautiful. The best work yet from a true American treasure'
Gary Shteyngart

'It takes an exceptional combination of moral humility and moral assurance to integrate fine-grained comedy and large-scale tragedy as daringly as Nathan Englander does. His writing is liberal in every good sense of the word' Jonathan Franzen

'Nathan Englander's new collection of stories tell the tangled truth of life, in prose that, as ever, surprises the reader with its gnarled beauty. One need look no further than 'Free Fruit for Young Widows' and 'Sister Hills' to find certifiable masterpieces of contemporary short story art'   Michael Chabon

'*What We Talk About When We Talk About Anne Frank* is Nathan Englander's wisest, funniest, bravest and most beautiful book. It overflows with revelations and gems'

Jonathan Safran Foer

'Nathan Englander's elegant, inquisitive, and hilarious fictions are a working definition of what the modern short story can do'
Jonathan Lethem

'Nathan Englander is one of our most consistently brilliant, bold and funny writers – that part isn't really in doubt – but the depth of his feeling is the thing that separates him from just about everyone. You can hear his heart thumping feverishly on every page. And his stories are perhaps the most ideal vessel for his gifts'   Dave Eggers

'This collection is a jolt of electricity through the heart, the head, the whole body nation. Here is a latitude of exquisitely wrought prose. Courageous and provocative. Edgy and timeless. In Englander's hands, story-telling is a transformative act. Put him alongside Singer, Carver and Munro. Englander is, quite simply, one of the very best we have'   Colum McCann

'Nathan Englander writes the stories I am always hoping for, searching for. These are stories that transport you into other lives, other dreams. This is deft, engrossing, deeply satisfying work. Englander is, to me, the modern master of the form. And this collection is the very best of the best'   Geraldine Brooks

'*What We Talk About When We Talk About Anne Frank* vividly displays the humor, complexity, and edge that we've come to expect from Nathan Englander's fiction – always animated by a deep, vibrant core of historical resonance'   Jennifer Egan

Nathan Englander is the author of the internationally bestselling story collection *For the Relief of Unbearable Urges* and the novel *The Ministry of Special Cases*. Translated into more than a dozen languages, Englander was selected as one of 20 Writers for the 21st Century by *The New Yorker* and has received a Guggenheim Fellowship, a PEN/Malamud Award, the Bard Fiction Prize, the Sue Kaufman Prize and the Frank O'Connor International Short Story Award. He lives in Brooklyn, New York.

www.nathanenglander.com

By Nathan Englander

For the Relief of Unbearable Urges
The Ministry of Special Cases
What We Talk About When We Talk About Anne Frank
Dinner at the Centre of the Earth

What We Talk About When We Talk About Anne Frank

Nathan Englander

WEIDENFELD & NICOLSON

A W&N PAPERBACK

First published in Great Britain in 2012
by Weidenfeld & Nicolson
This paperback edition published in 2013
by Weidenfeld & Nicolson,
an imprint of the Orion Publishing Group Ltd,
Carmelite House, 50 Victoria Embankment,
London EC4Y 0DZ

An Hachette UK company

5 7 9 10 8 6

A CIP catalogue record for this book
is available from the British Library.

ISBN 978-1-78022-229-5

Printed and bound in Great Britain
by Clays Ltd, St Ives plc

MIX
Paper from
responsible sources
FSC® C104740

www.orionbooks.co.uk

Contents

What We Talk About
When We Talk About
Anne Frank

They're in our house maybe ten minutes and already Mark's lecturing us on the Israeli occupation. Mark and Lauren live in Jerusalem, and people from there think it gives them the right.

Mark is looking all stoic and nodding his head. "If we had what you have down here in South Florida . . . ," he says, and trails off. "Yup," he says, and he's nodding again. "We'd have no troubles at all."

"You *do* have what we have," I tell him. "All of it. Sun and palm trees. Old Jews and oranges and the worst drivers around. At this point," I say, "we've probably got more Israelis than you." Debbie, my wife, she puts a hand on my arm. Her signal that I'm taking a tone, or interrupting someone's story, sharing something private, or making an inappropriate joke. That's my cue, and I'm surprised, considering how much I get it, that she ever lets go of my arm.

"Yes, you've got it all now," Mark says. "Even terrorists."

I look to Lauren. She's the one my wife has the relationship with—the one who should take charge. But Lauren isn't going to give her husband any signal. She and Mark ran off to Israel twenty years ago and turned Hassidic, and neither of them will put a hand on the other in public. Not for this. Not to put out a fire.

"Wasn't Mohamed Atta living right here before 9/11?" Mark says, and now he pantomimes pointing out houses. "Goldberg, Goldberg, Goldberg—Atta. How'd you miss him in this place?"

"Other side of town," I say.

"That's what I'm talking about. That's what you have that we don't. Other sides of town. Wrong sides of the tracks. Space upon space." And now he's fingering a granite countertop in our kitchen, looking out into the living room and the dining room, staring through the kitchen windows out at the pool. "All this house," he says, "and one son? Can you imagine?"

"No," Lauren says. And then she turns to us, backing him up. "You should see how we live with ten."

"Ten kids," I say. "We could get you a reality show with that here in the States. Help you get a bigger place."

The hand is back pulling at my sleeve. "Pictures," Debbie says. "I want to see the girls." We all follow Lauren into the den for her purse.

"Do you believe it?" Mark says. "Ten girls!" And the way it comes out of his mouth, it's the first time I like the guy. The first time I think about giving him a chance.

.   .   .

Facebook and Skype brought Deb and Lauren back together. They were glued at the hip growing up. Went to school together their whole lives. Yeshiva school. All girls. Out in Queens through high school and then riding the subway together to one called Central in Manhattan. They stayed best friends forever until I married Deb and turned her secular, and soon after that Lauren met Mark and they went off to the Holy Land and went from Orthodox to *ultra*-Orthodox, which to me sounds like a repackaged detergent—ORTHODOX ULTRA®, now with more deep-healing power. Because of that, we're supposed to call them Shoshana and Yerucham. Deb's been doing it. I'm just not saying their names.

"You want some water?" I offer. "Coke in the can?"

" 'You'—which of us?" Mark says.

"*You* both," I say. "I've got whiskey. Whiskey's kosher, too, right?"

"If it's not, I'll kosher it up real fast," he says, pretending to be easygoing. And right then, he takes off that big black hat and plops down on the couch in the den.

Lauren's holding the verticals aside and looking out at the yard. "Two girls from Forest Hills," she says. "Who ever thought we'd be the mothers of grown-ups?"

"Trevor's sixteen," Deb says. "You may think he's a grown-up, and he may think he's a grown-up—but we, we are not convinced."

"Well," Lauren says, "then whoever thought we'd have kids raised to think it's normal to have coconuts crashing out back and lizards climbing the walls?"

Right then is when Trev comes padding into the den, all six feet of him, plaid pajama bottoms dragging on the floor and T-shirt full of holes. He's just woken up and you can tell he's not sure if he's still dreaming. We told him we had guests. But there's Trev, staring at this man in the black suit, a beard resting on the middle of his stomach. And Lauren, I'd met her once before, right when Deb and I got married, but ten girls and a thousand Shabbos dinners later—well, she's a big woman, in a bad dress and a giant blond Marilyn Monroe wig. Seeing them at the door, I can't say I wasn't shocked myself. But the boy, he can't hide it on his face.

"Hey," he says.

And then Deb's on him, preening and fixing his hair and hugging him. "Trevy, this is my best friend from childhood," she says. "This is Shoshana, and this is—"

"Mark," I say.

"Yerucham," Mark says, and sticks out a hand. Trev shakes it. Then Trev sticks out his hand, polite, to Lauren. She looks at it, just hanging there in the air—offered.

"I don't shake," she says. "But I'm so happy to see you. Like meeting my own son. I mean it," she says. And here she starts to cry, for real. And she and Deb are hugging and Deb's crying, too. And the boys, we just stand there until Mark looks at his watch and gets himself a good manly grip on Trev's shoulder.

"Sleeping until three on a Sunday? Man, those were the days," Mark says. "A regular little Rumpleforeskin." Trev looks at me, and I want to shrug, but Mark's also looking, so I don't move. Trev just gives us both his best teenage glare and edges out of the room. As he does, he says, "Baseball practice," and takes my car keys off the hook by the door to the garage.

"There's gas," I say.

"They let them drive here at sixteen?" Mark says. "Insane."

. . .

"So what brings you," I say, "after all these years?" Deb's too far away to grab at me, but her face says it all. "Was I supposed to know?" I say. "Jeez, Deb must have told me. She told me, for sure. My fault."

"My mother," Mark says. "She's failing and my father's getting old—and they come to us for Sukkot every year. You know?"

"I know the holidays," I say.

"They used to fly out to us. For Sukkot and Pesach, both. But they can't fly now, and I just wanted to get over while things are still good. We haven't been in America—"

"Oh, gosh," Lauren says. "I'm afraid to think how long it's been. More than ten years. Twelve," she says. "Twelve years ago. With the kids, it's just impossible until enough of them are big. This might be"—and now she plops down on the couch—"this might be my first time in a house with no kids under the roof in that long. Oh my. I'm serious. How weird. I feel faint. And when I say *faint*," she says, standing up, giving an oddly girlish spin around, "what I mean is giddy."

"How do you do it?" Deb says. "Ten kids? I really do want to hear."

That's when I remember. "I forgot your drink," I say to Mark.

"Yes, his drink. That's how," Lauren says. "That's how we cope."

. . .

And that's how the four of us end up back at the kitchen table with a bottle of vodka between us. I'm not one to get drunk on a Sunday afternoon, but I tell you, with a plan to spend the day with Mark, I jump at the chance. Deb's drinking, too, but not for the same reason. For her and Lauren, I think they're reliving a little bit of the wild times. The very small window when they were together, barely grown-up, two young women living in New York on the edge of two worlds. And they just look, the both of them, so overjoyed to be reunited, I think they're half celebrating and half can't handle how intense the whole thing is.

Deb says, as she's already on her second, "This is really racy for us. I mean *really* racy. We try not to drink much at all these days. We think it sets a bad example for Trevor. It's not good to drink in front of them right at that age when they're all transgressive. He's suddenly so interested in that kind of thing."

"I'm just happy when he's interested in something," I say.

Deb slaps at the air. "I just don't think it's good to make drinking look like it's fun with a teenager around."

Lauren smiles and straightens her wig. "Does anything we do look fun to our kids?" I laugh at that. Honestly, I'm really liking her more and more.

"It's the age limit that does it," Mark says. "It's the whole American puritanical thing, the twenty-one-year-old drinking age and all that. We don't make a big deal about it in Israel, and so the kids, they don't even notice alcohol. Except for the foreign workers on Fridays, you hardly see anyone drunk at all."

"The workers and the Russians," Lauren says.

"The Russian immigrants," he says, "that's a whole separate matter. Most of them, you know, not even Jews."

"What does that mean?" I say.

"It means matrilineal descent, is what it means," Mark says. "It means with the Ethiopians there were conversions."

But Deb wants to keep us away from politics, and the way we're arranged, me in between them and Deb opposite (it's a round table, our kitchen table), she practically has to throw herself across to grab hold of my arm. "Fix me another," she says.

And here she switches the subject to Mark's parents. "How's the visit been going?" she says, her face all somber. "How are your folks holding up?"

Deb is very interested in Mark's parents. They're Holocaust survivors. And Deb has what can only be called an unhealthy obsession with the idea of that generation being gone. Don't get me wrong. It's important to me, too. I care, too. All I'm saying is, there's healthy and unhealthy, and my wife, she gives this subject a lot, *a lot,* of time. "Do you know," she'll say to me and Trevor, just absolutely out of nowhere, "World War Two veterans die at a rate of a thousand a day?"

"What can I say?" Mark says. "My mother's a very sick

woman. And my father, he tries to keep his spirits up. He's a tough guy."

"I'm sure," I say. And then I look in my drink, all serious, and give a shake of my head. "They really are amazing."

"Who?" Mark says. "Fathers?"

I look back up and they're all three staring at me. "Survivors," I say, seeing I jumped the gun.

"There's good and bad," Mark says. "Like anyone else." And then he laughs. "Though there isn't anyone else in my parents' place."

Lauren says, "You should see it. The whole of Carmel Lake Village, it's like a DP camp with a billiards room. They're all there."

"One tells the other," Marks says, "and they follow. It's amazing. From Europe to New York, and now, for the end of their lives, again the same place."

"Tell them that crazy story," Lauren says. "Tell them, Yuri."

"Tell us," Deb says. And I can see in her eyes that she wants it to be one of those stories of a guy who spent three years hiding inside one of those cannons they use for the circus. And at the end of the war, a Righteous Gentile comes out all joyous and fires him through a hoop and into a tub of water, where he discovers his lost son breathing through a straw.

"So you can picture my father," Mark says, "in the old country, he went to *heder*, had the *peyes* and all that. But in America, a classic *galusmonger*. He looks more like you than me. It's not from him that I get this," he says, pointing at his beard. "Shoshana and I—"

"We know," I say.

"So my father. They've got a nice nine-hole course, a driving range, some greens for the practice putting. And my dad, he's at the clubhouse. I go with him. He wants to work out in the gym, he says. Tells me I should come. Get some exercise. And he tells me"—and here Mark points at his feet, sliding a leg out from under the table so we can see his big black clodhoppers—"'You can't wear those Shabbos shoes on the treadmill. You need the sneakers. You know, sports shoes?' he says. And I tell him, 'I know what sneakers are. I didn't forget my English any more than your Yiddish is gone.' And so he says, *'Ah shaynem dank dir in pupik.'* Just to show me who's who."

"The point," Lauren says. "Tell them the point."

"So he's sitting in the locker room, trying to pull a sock on, which is, at that age, basically the whole workout in itself. It's no quick business. And I see, while I'm waiting, and I can't believe it. I nearly pass out. The guy next to him, the number on his arm, it's three before my father's number. You know, in sequence."

"What do you mean?" Deb says.

"I mean, the number tattooed. It's the same as my father's camp number, digit for digit, but my father's ends in an eight. And this guy's, it ends in a five. That's the only difference. I mean, they're separated by two people. And I look at this guy. I've never seen him before in my life. So I say, 'Excuse me, sir' to the guy. And he just says, 'You with the Chabad? I don't want anything but to be left alone. I already got candles at home.' I tell him, 'No. I'm not. I'm here visiting my father.' And to my father, I say, 'Do you know this gentleman? Have you two met? I'd really like to introduce you, if you haven't.' And they look each other over for what, I promise you, is minutes. Actual minutes. It is—with *kavod* I say this, with respect for my father— but it is like watching a pair of big beige manatees sitting on a bench, each with one sock on. They're just looking each other up and down, everything slow. And then my father says, 'I seen him. Seen him around.' The other guy, he says, 'Yes, I've seen.' 'You're both survivors,' I tell them. 'Look, look,' I say. 'The numbers.' And they look. 'They're the same,' I say. And they both hold out their arms to look at the little ashen tattoos. *'The same,'* I tell them. And to my father, I say, 'Do you get it? The same, except his—his, it's right ahead of yours. Look! Compare.' So they look. They compare." And to us now, Mark's eyes are popping out of his head. "I mean, think about it," he says. "Around the world, surviving the unsurvivable, these two old guys end up with enough money to retire to Carmel Lake and play golf every day. So I say to my dad, 'He's right ahead of you,' I say. 'Look, a five,' I say. 'And yours is an eight.' And the other guy looks and my father looks, and my father says, 'All that means is, he cut ahead of me in line. There, same as here. This guy's a cutter, I just didn't want to say.' 'Blow it out your ear,' the other guy says. And that's it. Then they get back to putting on socks."

Deb looks crestfallen. She was expecting something empowering. Some story with which to educate Trevor, to reconfirm her belief in the humanity that, from inhumanity, forms. So now she's just staring, her mouth hanging on to this thin, watery smile.

But me, I love that kind of story. I'm starting to take a real shine to both these two, and not just because I'm suddenly feeling sloshed.

"Good story, Yuri," I say, copying his wife. "Yerucham," I say, "that one's got zing."

Yerucham hoists himself up from the table, looking proud. He checks the label of our white bread on the counter—making sure it's kosher. He takes a slice, pulls off the crust, and rolls the white part against the countertop with the palm of his hand. He rolls it up into a little ball. He comes over and pours himself a shot and throws it back. And then he eats that crazy dough ball. Just tosses it in his mouth, as if it's the bottom of his own personal punctuation mark—you know, to underline his story.

"Is that good?" I say.

"Try it," he says. He goes to the counter and slings me, through the air, he pitches me a slice of white bread, and says, "But first pour yourself a shot."

I reach for the bottle and find that Deb's got her hands around it, and her head's bowed down, like the bottle is anchoring her, keeping her from tipping back.

"Are you okay, Deb?" Lauren says. She's got a hand on Deb's neck, and then switches to rubbing her arm. And I know what it is. I know what it is and I just up and say it: "It's because it was funny."

"Honey!" Deb says.

"She won't tell you, but she's a little obsessed with the Holocaust. And that story, no offense, Mark, it's not what she had in mind."

Mark is staring back and forth between us. And, honestly, the guy looks hurt. And I should leave it be, I know. But I just have to go on. It's not like someone from Deb's high school is around every day offering insights.

"It's like she's a survivor's kid, my wife. It's crazy, that education they give them. Her grandparents were all born in the Bronx, but it's like, I don't know. It's like here we are twenty minutes from downtown Miami, but really it's 1937 and we live on the edge of Berlin. It's astounding."

"That's not it!" Deb says, openly defensive, her voice just super high up on the register. "I'm not upset about that. It's just the alcohol. All this alcohol," she says, and rolls her eyes, making light. "It's that and seeing Lauren. Seeing Shoshana, after all this time."

"Oh, she was always like this in high school," Shoshana says. "Sneak one drink, and she started to cry."

"Alcohol is a known depressive," Yerucham says. And for that, for stating facts like that, he's straight on his way to being disliked again.

"You want to know what used to get her going, what would make her truly happy?" Shoshana says. And I tell you, I don't see it coming. I'm as blindsided as Deb was with that numbers story.

"It was getting high," Shoshana says. "That's what always did it. Smoking up, it would just make her laugh for hours and hours."

"Oh my God," Deb says, but not to Shoshana. She's pointing at me, likely because I look as startled as I feel. "Look at my big bad secular husband," Deb says. "He really can't handle it. He can't handle his wife's having any history of naughtiness at all—Mr. Liberal Open-Minded." And to me, she says, "How much more chaste a wife can you dream of than a modern-day Yeshiva girl who stayed a virgin until twenty-one? Honestly," she says, "what did you think Shoshana was going to say was so much fun?"

"Honestly-honestly?" I say. "I don't want to. It's embarrassing."

"Let's hear," Mark says. "We're all friends here. New friends, but friends."

"I thought you were—," I say, and I stop. "You'll kill me."

"Say it!" Deb says, positively glowing.

"Honestly, I thought you were going to say it was something like competing in the Passover Nut Roll, or making sponge cake. Something like that." I hang my head. And Shoshana and Deb are just laughing so hard, they can't breathe. They're grabbing at each other, so that I can't tell, really, if they're holding each other up or pulling each other down. I'm afraid one of them's going to fall.

"I can't believe you told him about the nut roll," Shoshana says.

"And I can't believe," Deb says, "you just told my husband of twenty-two years how much we used to get high. I haven't touched a joint since before we were married," she says. "Have we, honey? Have we smoked since we got married?"

"No," I say. "It's been a very long time."

"So, come on, Shosh. When was it? When was the last time you smoked?"

Now, I know I mentioned the beard on Mark. But I don't know if I mentioned how hairy a guy he is. It grows, that thing, right up to his eyeballs. Like having eyebrows on top and bottom both. It's really something. So when Deb asks the question, the two of them, Shosh and Yuri, they're basically giggling like children, and I can tell, in the little part that shows, in the bit of skin I can see, that Mark's eyelids and earlobes are in full blush.

"When Shoshana said we drink to get through the days," Mark says, "she was kidding about the drinking."

"We don't drink much," Shoshana says.

"It's smoking that she means," he says.

"We smoke," Lauren says, reconfirming.

"Cigarettes?" Deb says.

"We still get high," Shoshana says. "I mean, all the time."

"Hassidim!" Deb screams. "You're not allowed! There's no way."

"Everyone does in Israel. It's like the sixties there," Mark says. "Like a revolution. It's the highest country in the world. Worse than Holland, and India, and Thailand put together. Worse than anywhere, even Argentina—though they may have us tied."

"Well, maybe that's why the kids aren't interested in alcohol."

And Yerucham admits that maybe this is so.

"Do you want to get high now?" Deb says. And we all three look at her. Me, with surprise. And those two just with straight longing.

"We didn't bring," Shoshana says. "Though it's pretty rare anyone at customs peeks under the wig."

"Maybe you guys can find your way into the glaucoma underground over at Carmel Lake," I say. "I'm sure that place is rife with it."

"That's funny," Mark says.

"I'm funny," I say, now that we're all getting on.

"We've got pot," Deb says.

"We do?" I say. "I don't think we do."

Deb looks at me and bites at the cuticle on her pinkie.

"You're not secretly getting high all these years?" I say, feeling honestly like maybe I'm about to get a whole list of deceptions. I really don't feel well at all.

"Our son," Deb says. "He has pot."

"Our son?"

"Trevor," she says.

"Yes," I say. "I know which one."

. . .

It's a lot for one day, that kind of news. And it feels to me a lot like betrayal. Like my wife's old secret and my son's new secret are wound up together and that I've somehow been wronged. Also, I'm not one to recover quickly from any kind of slight from Deb—not when there are other people around. I really need to talk stuff out. Some time alone with Deb, even five minutes, would fix it. But it's super-apparent that she doesn't need any time alone with me. She doesn't seem troubled at all. What she seems is focused. She's busy at the counter, using a paper tampon wrapper to roll up a joint.

"It's an emergency preparedness method we came up with in high school," Shoshana says. "The things teenage girls will do when they're desperate."

"And we were desperate," Deb says, as if everything's already funny. "Do you remember that nice boy from Y.H.S.Q. that we used to smoke in front of?"

"I can picture him," Shoshana says. "But not the name."

"He'd just watch us," Deb says. "There'd be six or seven of us in a circle, girls and boys not touching—we were so religious. Isn't that crazy?" Deb is talking to me, as Shoshana and Mark don't think it's crazy at all. "The only place we touched was passing the joint, at the thumbs. And this boy, we had a nickname for him."

" 'Passover'!" Shoshana yells.

"Yes," Deb says, "that's it. All we ever called him was 'Passover.' Because every time the joint got to him, he'd just pass it over to the next one. Passover Rand," Deb says. "Now I remember."

Shoshana takes the joint and lights it with a match, sucking in deep. "It's a miracle when I remember anything these days," she says. "I'm telling you. It's the kids. After my first was born, I forgot half of everything I knew. And then half again with each one after. Ten kids later, it's amazing when I remember to blow out a match after I light it." She drops the one she's holding into the sink, and it makes that little hiss. "Just last night, I woke up in a panic. I couldn't remember if there were fifty-two cards in a deck or fifty-two weeks in a year. The recall errors—I'm up all night worrying over them, just waiting for the Alzheimer's to kick in."

"It's not that bad," Mark tells her. "It's only everyone on one side of your family that has it."

"That's true," she says, passing her husband the joint. "The other side is blessed only with dementia. Anyway, which is it? Weeks or cards?"

"Same, same," Mark says, taking a hit.

When it's Deb's turn, she holds the joint and looks at me,

like I'm supposed to nod or give her permission in some husbandly anxiety-absolving way. And I just can't take it anymore. Instead of saying, "Go ahead," or "Let's do it," I pretty much bark at Deb. "When were you going to tell me about our son?" I say. "When was that going to happen? How long have you known?"

At that, Deb takes a long hit, and holds it deep, like an old pro.

"Really, Deb. How could you not tell me you knew?"

Deb walks over and hands me the joint. She blows the smoke in my face, not aggressive, just blowing.

"I've only known five days," she says. "I was going to tell you, obviously. I just wasn't sure how, or if I should talk to Trevy first, maybe give him a chance," she says.

"A chance to what?" I ask.

"To let him keep it as a secret between us. To let him know he could have my trust, could be forgiven, if he promised to stop."

"But he's the son," I say. "I'm the father. Even if it's a secret with him, it should be a double secret between me and you. I should always get to know—but pretend not to know—any secret with him."

"Do that double part again," Mark says, trying to follow. But I ignore him.

"That's how it goes," I say to Deb. "That's how it's always been." And because I'm desperate and unsure, I follow it up with "Hasn't it?"

I mean, we really trust each other, Deb and I. And I can't remember feeling like so much has hung on one question in a long, long time. I'm trying to read her face, and something really complex is going on, some formulation. And then she just sits right there on the floor at my feet.

"Oh my God," she says. "I'm so fucking high. Like instantly.

Like, like," and then she starts laughing. "Like, Mike," she says. "Like, kike," she says, turning completely serious. "Oh my God, I'm really messed up."

"We should have warned you," Shoshana says.

As she says this, I'm holding my first hit in, and already trying to fight off the paranoia that comes rushing behind that statement. Mark takes the joint back and passes it straight to Shoshana, respecting the order of things.

"Warn us what?" I say, my voice high, and the smoke still sweet in my nose.

"This isn't your father's marijuana," he says. "The THC levels. It's like, I don't know, the stuff from our childhood? One hit of this new hydroponic stuff, it's like if maybe you smoked a pound of the stuff we had when we were kids."

"I feel it," I say. And I do, in a deep, deep way. And I sit down with Deb on the floor and take her hands. I feel nice. Though I'm not sure if I thought that or said it, so I try it again, making sure it's out loud. "I feel nice," I say.

"I found it in the laundry hamper," Deb says. "That's where I got the pot."

"In the hamper?" Shoshana says.

"Leave it to a teenage boy to think that's the best place to hide something," Deb says. "His clean clothes show up folded in his room, and it never occurs to him that someone empties the hamper. To him, it's the loneliest, most forgotten space in the world. Point is," Deb says, "I found an Altoids tin at the bottom, stuffed full. Just brimming with pot." Deb gives my hands a squeeze. "Are we good now?"

"We're good," I say. And it feels like we're a team again, like it's us against them. Because when Shoshana passes Deb the joint, Deb says, "Are you sure you guys are allowed to smoke pot that comes out of a tin that held non-kosher candy? I really don't know if that's okay." And it's just exactly the kind of thing I'm thinking right then.

"She's on Facebook, too," I say. "That can't be allowed, either. These are very bad Hassidim," I say, and we laugh at that. We laugh hard.

"First of all, we're not eating it. We're smoking it. And even so, it's cold contact, so it's probably all right either way," Shoshana says.

"'Cold contact?'" I say.

"It's a thing," Shoshana says. "Just forget about it and get up off the floor. Chop-chop." And each of them offers us a hand and gets us standing. "Come, sit back at the table," Shoshana says. So once we're up, we're back down again at the table.

"I'll tell you," Mark says. "That's got to be the number-one most annoying thing about being Hassidic in the outside world. Worse than the rude stuff that gets said is the constant policing by civilians. I'm telling you, everywhere we go, people are checking on us. Ready to make some sort of liturgical citizen's arrest."

"Strangers!" Shoshana says. "Just the other day, down here, on the way from the airport. Yuri pulled into a McDonald's to pee, and some guy in a trucker hat came up to him as he went in and said, 'You allowed to go in there, brother?' Just like that."

"Not true!" Deb says.

"True," Shoshana says.

"It's not that I don't see the fun in that," Mark says. "The allure. You know, we've got Mormons in Jerusalem. They've got a base there. A seminary. The rule is—the deal with the government—they can have their place, but they can't do outreach. No proselytizing. Anyway, I do some business with one of their guys."

"From Utah?" Deb says.

"From Idaho. His name is Jebediah, for real—do you believe it?"

"No, Yerucham and Shoshana," I say. "Jebediah is a very strange name." Mark rolls his eyes at that, and hands me what's left of the joint. Without even asking, he gets up and gets the tin and reaches into his wife's purse for another tampon. He's confident now, at home in my home. And I'm a little less comfortable with this than with the white bread, with a guest coming into the house and smoking up all our son's pot. Deb must be thinking something similar, as she says, "After this story, I'm going to text Trev and make sure he's not coming back anytime soon."

"That'd be good," I say.

"Actually, I'll tell him to come straight home after practice. Or I'll tell him he can have dinner with his friends but that he better be here by nine, not a minute later. Then he'll beg for ten. If I tell him he has to be home no matter what, we're safe."

"Okay," I say. "A good plan."

"So when Jeb's at our house, when he comes by to eat and pours himself a Coke, I do that same religious-police thing. I can't resist. I say, 'Hey, Jeb, you allowed to have that? You supposed to be drinking Coke, or what?' I say it every time. Somehow, I can't resist. People don't mind breaking their own rules, but they're real strict about someone else's."

"So are they allowed to have Coke?" Deb says.

"I don't know," Mark says. "All Jeb ever says back is, 'You're thinking of coffee, and mind your own business, either way.'"

"What happens in Jerusalem, stays in Jerusalem," I say. But they must not have that commercial there, because neither of them thinks that's funny at all.

And then my Deb. She just can't help herself. "You heard about the scandal? The Mormons going through the Holocaust list."

"Like in *Dead Souls*," I say, explaining, "Like in the Gogol book, but real."

"Do you think we read that?" Mark says. "As Hassidim, or before?" He passes me the joint as he says this, so it's both a little aggressive and funny at the same time. And then, because one doesn't preclude the other, he pours himself a drink.

"They took the records of the dead," Deb says, "and they started running through them. They took these people who died as Jews and started converting them into Mormons. Converting the six million against their will."

"And this bothers you?" Mark says. "This is what keeps an American Jew up at night?"

"What does that mean?" Deb says.

"It means—," Mark says.

But Shoshana interrupts him. "Don't tell them what it means, Yuri. Just leave it unmeant."

"We can handle it," I say. "We are interested, even, in handling it. This stuff," I say, pointing in the general direction of the Altoids tin, "has ripened our minds. We're primed to entertain even the highest concepts."

"High concepts, because we're high," Deb says, earnest, not joking at all.

"Your son, he seems like a nice boy."

"Do not talk about their son," Shoshana says.

"Do not talk about our son," Deb says. This time I reach across and lay a hand on her elbow.

"Talk," I say.

"He does not," Mark says, "seem Jewish to me."

"How can you say that?" Deb says. "What is wrong with you?" But Deb's upset draws less attention than my response. I am laughing so hard that everyone turns toward me.

"What?" Mark says.

"Jewish to you?" I say. "The hat, the beard, the blocky shoes. A lot of pressure, I'd venture, to look Jewish to you. Like say, maybe, Ozzy Osbourne, or the guys from Kiss, like them telling Paul Simon, saying, 'You do not look like a musician to me.'"

"It is not about the outfit," Mark says. "It's about building life in a vacuum. Do you know what I saw on the drive over here? Supermarket, supermarket, adult bookstore, supermarket, supermarket, firing range."

"Floridians do like their guns and porn," I say. "And their supermarkets."

"Oh my God," Deb says. "That's like your 'Goldberg, Goldberg—Atta' thing. Just the same, but different words."

"He likes that rhythm," Shoshana says. "He does that a lot."

"What I'm trying to say, whether you want to take it seriously or not, is that you can't build Judaism only on the foundation of one terrible crime. It is about this obsession with the Holocaust as a necessary sign of identity. As your only educational tool. Because for the children, there is no connection otherwise. Nothing Jewish that binds."

"Wow, that's offensive," Deb says. "And close-minded. There is such a thing as Jewish culture. One can live a culturally rich life."

"Not if it's supposed to be a Jewish life. Judaism is a religion. And with religion comes ritual. Culture is nothing. Culture is some construction of the modern world. And because of that, it is not fixed; it is ever-changing, and a weak way to bind generations. It's like taking two pieces of metal, and instead of making a nice weld, you hold them together with glue."

"What does that even mean?" Deb says. "Practically."

Mark raises a finger to make his point, to educate. "Do you know why in Israel all the buses and trucks, why all the taxis, even, are Mercedes?"

"Because they give you a big guilt-based discount?" I say. "Or maybe because Mercedes is the best at building vehicles for the transport of Jews—they have a certain knack?"

"Because in Israel we are sound, solid Jews, and so it is nothing, even right after the war, for us to drive German cars and turn on our German Siemens radios to listen to the Hebrew news. We don't need to impose some brand-based apartheid, to busy ourselves with symbolic efforts to keep our memories in place. Because we live exactly as our parents lived before the war. And this serves us in all things, in our relationships, too, in our marriages and parenting."

"Are you saying your marriage is better than ours?" Deb says. "Really? Just because of the rules you live by? That makes a marriage stronger—just between any two random people?"

"I'm saying your husband would not have the long face, worried over if his wife is keeping secrets. And your son, he would not get into the business of smoking without first coming to you. Because the relationships, they are defined. They are clear."

"Because they are welded together," I say, "and not glued."

"Yes," he says. "And I bet Shoshana agrees." But Shoshana is distracted. She is working carefully with an apple and a knife. She is making a little apple pipe, all the tampons done.

"Did your daughters?" Deb says. "If they tell you everything, did they come to you first, before they smoked?"

"Our daughters do not have the taint of the world we grew up in. They have no interest in such things."

"So you think," I say.

"So I know," he says. "Our concerns are different, our worries."

"Let's hear 'em," Deb says.

"Let's not," Shoshana says. "Honestly, we're drunk, we're high, we are having a lovely reunion."

"Every time you tell him not to talk," I say, "it makes me want to hear what he's got to say more."

"Our concern," Mark says, "is not the past Holocaust. It is the current one. The one that takes more than fifty percent of the Jews this generation. Our concern is intermarriage. It is the Holocaust that's happening now. You don't need to be worrying about some Mormons doing hocus-pocus on the murdered six million. You need to worry that your son marries a Jew."

"Oh my God," Deb says. "Oh my God. Are you calling intermarriage a Holocaust? You can't really—I mean, Shoshana. I mean, don't . . . Are you really comparing?"

"You ask my feeling, that's my feeling. But this, no, it does not exactly apply to you, except in the example you set for the boy. Because you're Jewish, your son, he is as Jewish as me. No more, no less."

"I went to yeshiva, too, Born-Again Harry! You don't need to explain the rules to me."

"Did you call me 'Born-Again Harry'?" Mark asks.

"I did," Deb says. And she and he, they start to laugh at that. They think "Born-Again Harry" is the funniest thing they've heard in awhile. And Shoshana then laughs, and then I laugh, because laughter is infectious—and it is doubly so when you're high.

"You don't really think our family, my lovely, beautiful son, is headed for a Holocaust, do you?" Deb says. "Because that would really hurt. That would really cast a pall on this beautiful day."

"No, I don't," Mark says. "It is a lovely house and a lovely family, a beautiful home that you've made for that strapping young man. You're a real *balabusta*," Mark says. "I mean it."

"That makes me happy," Deb says. And she tilts her head

nearly ninety degrees to show her happy, sweet smile. "Can I hug you?" Deb says. "I'd really like to give you a hug."

"No," Mark says, though he says it really, really politely. "But you can hug my wife. How about that?"

"That's a great idea," Deb says. Shoshana hands the loaded apple to me, and I smoke from the apple as the two women hug a tight, deep, dancing-back-and-forth hug, tilting this way and that, so, once again, I'm afraid they might fall.

"It is a beautiful day," I say.

"It is," Mark says. And both of us look out the window, and both of us watch the perfect clouds in a perfect sky. We are watching this and enjoying this, and so we are staring out, too, as the sky darkens in an instant. It is a change so abrupt that the ladies undo their hug to watch, so sharp is the sudden change of light.

"It is like that here," Deb says. And then the skies open up and torrential tropical rain drops straight down, battering. It is loud against the roof, and loud against the windows, and the fronds of the palm trees bend, and the floaties in the pool jump as the water boils.

Shoshana goes to the window. And Mark passes Deb the apple and goes to the window. "Really, it's always like this here?" Shoshana says.

"Sure," I say. "Every day like that. Stops as quick as it starts."

And both of them have their hands pressed up against the window. And they stay like that for some time, and when Mark turns around, harsh guy, tough guy, we see that he is weeping. Weeping from the rain.

"You do not know," he says. "I forget what it's like to live in a place rich with water. This is a blessing above all others."

"If you had what we had," I say.

"Yes," he says, wiping his eyes.

"Can we go out?" Shoshana says. "In the rain?"

"Of course," Deb says. And then Shoshana tells me to close my eyes. To close them tight. Only me. And I swear, I think she's going to be stark naked when she calls, "Open up."

She's taken off her wig is all, and she's wearing one of Trev's baseball hats in its place.

"I've only got the one wig this trip," she says. "If Trev wouldn't mind."

"He wouldn't mind," Deb says. And this is how the four of us move out into the rain. How we find ourselves in the backyard, on a searingly hot day, getting pounded by all this cool, cool rain. It is, with the weather, and the being high, and being drunk, and after all that conversation, it is just about the best feeling in the world. And I have to say, Shoshana looks twenty years younger in that hat.

We do not talk. We are too busy frolicking and laughing and jumping around. And that's how it happens, that I'm holding Mark's hand and sort of dancing, and Deb is holding Shoshana's hand, and also, they're doing their own kind of jig. And when I take Deb's hand, though neither of those two is touching the other, somehow we've formed a broken circle. We've started dancing our own kind of hora in the rain.

It is the most glorious, and silliest, and freest I can remember feeling in years. Who would think that's what I'd be saying with these strict, suffocatingly austere people come to visit our house. And then my Deb, my love, once again she is thinking what I'm thinking and she says, face up into the rain, all of us spinning, "Are you sure this is okay, Shoshana? That it's not mixed dancing? That this is allowed? I don't want anyone feeling bad after."

"We'll be just fine," Shoshana says. "We will live with the

consequences." The question slows us, and stops us, though no one has yet let go.

"It's like the old joke," I say. And without waiting for anyone to ask which one, I say, "Why don't Hassidim have sex standing up?"

"Why?" Shoshana says.

"Because it might lead to mixed dancing."

Deb and Shoshana pretend to be horrified as we let go of hands, as we recognize that the moment is over, the rain disappearing as quickly as it came. Mark stands there staring into the sky, lips pressed tight. "That joke is very, very old," he says. And then he says, "Mixed dancing makes me think of mixed nuts, and mixed grill, and *insalata mista*. The sound of 'mixed dancing' has made me wildly hungry. And I'm going to panic if the only kosher thing in the house is that loaf of bleached American bread."

"You have the munchies," I say.

"Diagnosis correct," he says.

Deb starts clapping at that, tiny claps, her hands held to her chest in prayer. "You will not," Deb says to him, absolutely beaming, "even believe what riches await."

.   .   .

The four of us stand in the pantry, soaking wet, hunting through the shelves and dripping on the floor. "Have you ever seen such a pantry?" Shoshana says. "It's gigantic," she says, reaching her arms out from side to side. It is indeed large, and it is indeed stocked, an enormous amount of food, and an enormous selection of sweets, befitting a home that is often host to a swarm of teenage boys.

"Are you expecting a nuclear winter?" Shoshana says.

"I'll tell you what she's expecting," I say. "You want to know how obsessed she really is? You want to understand how much she truly talks about the Holocaust? I mean, how serious it is—to what degree?"

"To no degree," Deb says. "We are done with the Holocaust."

"Tell us," Shoshana says.

"She's always plotting our secret hiding place," I say.

"No kidding," Shoshana says.

"Like, look at this. At the pantry, and a bathroom next to it, and the door to the garage. If you just sealed it all up—like put drywall at the entrance to the den—you'd never know. You'd never suspect. If you covered that door inside the garage up good with, I don't know, if you hung your tools in front of it and hid hinges behind, maybe leaned the bikes and the mower up against it, you'd have this closed area, with running water and a toilet and all this food. I mean, if someone sneaked into the garage to replenish things, you could rent out the house, you know? Put in another family without even any idea."

"Oh my God," Shoshana says. "My short-term memory may be gone from having all those children—"

"And from the smoking," I say.

"And from that, too. But I remember. I remember from when we were kids, she was always," Shoshana says, turning to Deb, "you were always getting me to play games like that. To pick out spaces. And even worse, even darker—"

"Don't," Deb says.

"I know what you're going to say," I tell her, and I'm honestly excited. "The game, yes? She played that crazy game with you?"

"No," Deb says. "Enough. Let it go."

And Mark—who is just utterly absorbed in studying kosher certifications, who is tearing through hundred-calorie snack packs and eating handfuls of roasted peanuts from a jar, and who has said nothing since we entered the pantry except "What's a Fig Newman?"—he stops and says, "I want to play this game."

"It's not a game," Deb says.

And I'm happy to hear her say that, as that's just what I've been trying to get her to admit for years. That it's not a game. That it's dead serious, and a kind of preparation, and an active pathology that I prefer not to indulge.

"It's the Anne Frank game," Shoshana says. "Right?"

Seeing how upset my wife is, I do my best to defend her. I say, "No, it's not a game. It's just what we talk about when we talk about Anne Frank."

"How do we play this non-game?" Mark says. "What do we do?"

"It's the Righteous Gentile game," Shoshana says.

"It's Who Will Hide Me?" I say.

"In the event of a second Holocaust," Deb says, giving in, speaking tentatively. "It's a serious exploration, a thought experiment that we engage in."

"That you play," Shoshana says.

"That, in the event of an American Holocaust, we sometimes talk about which of our Christian friends would hide us."

"I don't get it," Mark says.

"Of course you do," Shoshana says. "You absolutely do. It's like this. If there was a Shoah, if it happened again, say we were in Jerusalem, and it's 1941 and the Grand Mufti got his way, what would your friend Jebediah do?"

"What could he do?" Mark says.

"He could hide us. He could risk his life and his family's and everyone's around him. That's what the game is: Would he—for real—would he do that for you?"

"He'd be good for that, a Mormon," Mark says. "Forget

this pantry. They have to keep a year of food stored in case of the Rapture, or something like that. Water, too. A year of supplies. Or maybe it's that they have sex through a sheet. No, wait," Mark says, "I think that's supposed to be us."

"All right," Deb says, "let's not play. Really, let's go back to the kitchen. I can order in from the glatt kosher place. We can eat outside on the grass, and have a real dinner and not just junk."

"No, no," Mark says, "I'll play. I'll take it seriously."

"So would the guy hide you?" I say.

"And the kids, too?" Mark says. "I'm supposed to pretend that in Jerusalem he's got a hidden motel or something where he can put the twelve of us?"

"Yes," Shoshana says. "In their seminary or something. Sure."

Mark thinks about this for a long, long time. He eats Fig Newmans and considers, and you can tell from the way he's staring that he's gotten into it, that he's taking it real seriously—serious to the extreme.

"Yes," Mark says, and he looks honestly choked up. "I think, yes, Jeb would do that for us. He would hide us. He would risk it all."

"I think so, too," Shoshana says, and smiles. "Wow, it makes you—as an adult—it makes you appreciate people more."

"Yes," Mark says. "Jeb's a good man."

"Now you go," Shoshana says to us. "You take a turn."

"But we don't know any of the same people anymore," Deb says. "We usually just talk about the neighbors."

"Our across-the-street neighbors," I tell them. "They're the perfect example. Because the husband, Mitch, he would hide us. I know it. He'd lay down his life for what's right. But that wife of his . . ." I say.

"Yes," Deb says, "he's right. Mitch would hide us, but

Gloria, she'd buckle. When he was at work one day, she'd turn us in."

"You could play against yourselves, then," Shoshana says. "What if one of you wasn't Jewish? Would you hide the other?"

"I'll do it," I say. "I'll be the Gentile, because I could pass best. A grown woman who still has an ankle-length denim skirt in her closet—they'd catch you in a flash."

"Fine," Deb says. And I stand up straight, put my shoulders back, like maybe I'm in a lineup. I stand there with my chin raised so my wife can study me. So she can really get a look in, and get a think in, and decide if her husband really has what it takes. Would I really have the strength, would I care enough—and it is not a light question, not a throwaway question—to risk my life to save her and our son?

Deb stares, and Deb smiles, and gives me a little push to my chest. "Of course he would," Deb says. And she takes the half stride that's between us and gives me a tight hug that she doesn't release. "Now you," Deb says. "You and Yuri go."

"How does that even make sense?" Mark says. "Even for imagining."

"Shhh," Shoshana says. "Just stand over there and be a good Gentile while I look."

"But if I weren't Jewish, I wouldn't be me."

"That's for sure," I say.

"He agrees," Mark says. "We wouldn't even be married. We wouldn't have kids."

"Of course you can imagine it," Shoshana says. "Look," she says, and goes over and closes the pantry door. "Here we are, caught in South Florida for the second Holocaust. You're not Jewish, and you've got the three of us hiding in your pantry."

"But look at me!" he says.

"I've got a fix," I say. "You're a background singer for ZZ Top. You know them? You know that band?"

Deb lets go of me, just so she can give my arm a slap.

"Really," Shoshana says. "Try to look at the three of us like that, like it's your house and we're your charges, locked up in this room."

"And what're you going to do while I do that?" Mark says.

"I'm going to look at you looking at us. I'm going to imagine."

"Okay," he says. "*Nu*, get to it. I will stand, you imagine."

And that's what we do, the four of us. We stand there playing our roles, and we really get into it. We really all imagine it. I can see Deb seeing him, and him seeing us, and Shoshana just staring and staring at her husband.

We stand there so long, I really can't tell how much time has passed, though the light changes ever so slightly—the sun outside again dampening—in that crack under the pantry door.

"So would I hide you?" he says, serious. And for the first time that day, he reaches out, as my Deb would, and puts his hand to her hand. "Would I, Shoshi?"

And you can tell Shoshana is thinking of her kids, though that's not part of the scenario. You can tell that she's changed part of the imagining. And she says, after a pause, yes, but she's not laughing. She says, yes, but to him it sounds as it does to us, so that he is now asking and asking. But wouldn't I? Wouldn't I hide you? Even if it was life and death—if it would spare you, and they'd kill me alone for doing it? Wouldn't I?

Shoshana pulls back her hand.

She does not say it. And he does not say it. And from the four of us, no one will say what cannot be said—that this wife believes her husband would not hide her. What to do? What would come of it? And so we stand like that, the four of us trapped in that pantry. Afraid to open the door and let out what we've locked inside.

Sister Hills

I: 1973

On a hilltop not many miles east of Jerusalem, Hanan Cohen watched the dust rising up in the distance and knew they were having a war. The roads remain empty on the Day of Atonement, and the cloud from a convoy barreling down toward the desert could mean only one thing. Hanan put a hand to his eyes to block the sun, hoping to see better. Holding that position, with his beard blowing, and his long white robe, and the tallit on his shoulders, he looked—poised among those ancient hills—like a man outside of time.

He walked back into the one-room shack where he lived with his wife and his three teenage sons. He undressed, put on his uniform, and took up his gun so that no one needed to ask what he had seen.

The boys said, "We will come, too. There will be some way to help."

"Stay with your mother," Hanan said.

And Rena, who did not need her husband to make such a decision, said, "Follow your father to the city, and see if there's any way you may serve your country in its time of need."

Hanan nodded, accepting. And he, along with his three boys, walked out toward the war.

. . .

Rena did not sleep that night, worried as she was for her husband and her sons. The worry was made worse by the newness of the place and its simplicity. Centered in the middle of an olive grove, the shack was without running water or electricity. Whatever radio signal wasn't swallowed by the surrounding mountains was blocked by the trees. A home so rustic wasn't wired for a phone.

When Rena broke her fast after dark, she thought about hiking down across the little valley out her front door and climbing the hill on the other side. For on that other small summit sat another shack, with another family. The only Jews for miles around. In it lived a husband and wife and their new baby daughter. The husband, Skote, was a friend of Hanan's, and together they'd come up with the plan, and bought the land, and decided to settle this area of Samaria together, and build from their two families a great and mighty city on that place.

Rena figured that Skote, too, had seen the dust. And that, most sensibly, Yehudit had taken her baby daughter and followed her husband to the closest road when he'd left to join the fight. Rena sincerely hoped that's what she'd done. At the best of times, this was not a safe place to be alone. There was a walkie-talkie in the shack, and Rena called out to Yehudit, but heard nothing on any of the channels, only broken flashes, like lightning, of passing chatter. Rena decided against crossing. She didn't want to find herself alone on the opposite hilltop, only to have to make her way back in the night.

Rena sat with her back to the door and her eyes to the window. She recited psalms with her rifle in her lap, and watched for any movement that might be headed up her hill. She stayed this way until morning, frightened countless times by the rustling of leaves on stiff branches. And more so, she was terrified by what she could not see, the ever-widening gyre of frontier blocked by the tree at her window.

. . .

After washing her hands and saying her prayers, Rena went outside with the ax to size up the task ahead. It was the biggest tree in their grove, a solid four meters around. Then she looked up to its top and knew she could conquer it. For the tree, like the men of that country, was much shorter than you'd imagine for something so tough. Rena spat in her hands. She took up her ax, and she swung at the tree's knobbly base with all she had. She chopped and chopped, making little progress. When she was feeling forlorn, too tired to hack at that stubborn bole anymore, she'd look out past the tree over the edge of the hill at the Arab village below. And she'd swing.

Watching this handsome mother of three at work, her hair tied back in a kerchief, and reigning over this stunning hill, in a sea of hills, on a day so clear that one could see well into the purple mountains of Moab from where Rena stood, you would not know that things weighed heavy at all. You would not know it if, upon taking her periodic look over the edge of that rocky slope and spotting a skinny young man climbing its worn, ancient terraces, she hadn't buried that ax in the ground and lifted a rifle from the dirt.

Rena chambered a round. She planted the butt on her shoulder and set her sights on the boy zigzagging his way up. When he was close enough to Rena that she could have as easily poked him back down the hill with the barrel as shot him through the heart, he said, in Arabic, "Stop chopping my tree."

Rena either didn't speak Arabic or didn't care to respond. And so the boy repeated the sentence in Hebrew.

Again, it was as if he had not spoken. Rena, as if starting the conversation, said, "Who are you?"

"I am," he said, "your neighbor down the hill."

"Then stay down the hill," she said.

"I would have," the boy said. "But I looked up and I saw that you were doing something that can't be undone."

"It's my tree, on my land, in my country. Mine to cut down if I please."

"If it was your tree, I'd have seen you at my side last year during harvest. I'd have seen you the year before that, and ten years before that, and a hundred."

"You weren't here yourself a hundred years ago. And anyway," Rena said, "you don't look back far enough. The contract on this land is very old."

"A mythical claim, as meaningless as the one you make today."

Here the boy went silent as the shadows from a formation of fighters passed overhead. Then he waited a moment longer, for he knew they would be followed by the crack of broken sky.

"You will see," the boy said. "The Jewish court will return this hill to us. Anyway, it looks like it's the war, not a judge, that will decide. Tomorrow, I'd say, or the next, this tree will be in Jordan, or Egypt, or, God willing, back home in Palestine."

"By tomorrow," Rena said, "it will be at the bottom of the hill. And you can take it, along with your family, to any country you please."

Here the boy's face darkened, as if a plane again had passed, though the sky stayed clear.

"If I find one single olive branch off this tree at the bottom of the hill," he said, a finger now raised, "I will plant you in its place myself. One more swing, I tell you, and a curse on your head—a curse on your home."

"You are very tough for a boy with a gun aimed at his heart."

"A settler who shoots for no reason would already have shot."

And here the boy turned and walked back down the hill. He was halfway down when Rena called to him, against her better judgment. "Child," she yelled. "Cousin! Are we really losing the war?"

. . .

Rena chopped at that tree for the rest of the morning. With each swing, she thought of the boy's curse, and the boy's threat, and wondered, if she felled the tree that day, if he'd really come for her that night. But that tree was a dense tree. And her ax needed sharpening. And as strong as she was, her arms would need strengthening, or at least a night of rest, to get the job done. When she knew she could not finish, Rena went back into the shack. She cleared her mug and plate from the table and tipped it onto its side. She then flipped it up against the window to act as a shutter, and turned her chair around to face the other side of the room. Rena sat with her back to the window, the gun in her lap, and her eyes set on a door so flimsy that when night came, she was able to see the stars through the gaps in its boards.

Deep into that night, there was a banging at the door that Rena was sure was the boy from the village come to get her. Cloudy with sleep, she was up in an instant, the gun at her shoulder, her finger on the trigger, and squeezing so hard in her fright that there was no way to stop it, when she remembered it might be her husband or her sons coming home. In that very same instant, for it was too small to split, she pitched up the barrel and shot a tile from her roof.

Rena heard her neighbor Yehudit scream on the other side of that door. She ran to open it, saying a dozen prayers at once, thankful she had not killed her friend. When Yehudit was safely inside with her baby, and the bolt slid back into place, Rena set the hive of a lantern to glowing and held it out to the woman before her. And she saw that the baby Yehudit carried did not sit right in her arms. From the way she held it, Rena assumed that the child was already dead.

"Is she—" Rena said.

"Sick," Yehudit said. "A thousand degrees. I tried every remedy, said every prayer." And then, in the middle of her panic, she said, "Why did we move to this place? By whose call does it fall on us to rebuild this nation? Two families alone among olives and enemies. I said to Skote before all of this, 'What if there is an emergency, and us cut off, no phones, no roads, only hills around? What if something happens after the baby is born?'"

"Do you want me to hike down with you?" Rena said, looking for a clock. "We can be at the crossing before the sun comes up."

"It's too far and too dangerous. And you can see already, the decision about this child's life will be made tonight."

"Let me hold her," Rena said. And she took the child, who was hot as white coal. Her lips were cracked deep and peeling like parchment, her little eyes dry and dead. Rena did not think this child could be saved. She handed the baby back to its mother, and took up the blanket that was folded on her cot.

"What are you doing?" Yehudit said.

"Making you a place to rest, so that I can care for the baby while you sleep. We will take turns nursing her through the night."

"I didn't come for company. I didn't come to stay."

"Well, what can I do that you haven't already done?"

"You can buy the child."

"What?" Rena said.

"In the way of the old country—to outsmart what's coming. It's how my own grandmother was saved from the Angel of Death."

"I'll recite psalms with you until the pages turn to dust," Rena said, "but superstition and magic?"

Yehudit put a hand to the back of the baby's head and turned away the shoulder on which the child rested, as if Rena herself were possibly Death in another guise.

"You don't see it?" Yehudit said. "Why else, on Yom Kippur, would God call my husband away to war? To do that, and then reach into my home to take back the blessing He'd just sent me? And this after I've left behind my whole family. This after I moved up to a forgotten hilltop, after I sacrificed happiness to make Israel whole. No, there has been a sin. There has been some evil of which I'm unaware. But it is my evil. This child, alone out here, utterly pure."

"And you think selling your baby will break a fever that hot."

"If she were not my child anymore," Yehudit said, "if she meant so little to me that I'd sell her for a pittance. If she belonged, in earnest, to another mother, then maybe those forces that take interest would see that it is not worth the bother. And if she is truly no longer my child," Yehudit said, owning whatever dark cloud hovered over her, "maybe whatever's coming won't even know where to look."

Rena nodded, accepting. She rummaged through a vegetable crate full of books for the one in which she and Hanan hid their money. She took out a stack of bills. This she offered to Yehudit, who took one worthless note off the top. *"Shtei pru-*

tot," Yehudit said. "I won't take more money for her than I would for a loaf a bread." Yehudit then gave that bill back to Rena and straightened herself, preparing for the exchange.

"I declare this child to be a daughter of this house," Yehudit said. "I make no claim to her anymore." She passed that boiling baby over to Rena, and in return took that single bill in her hand. "I ask only," Yehudit said, "that you consider one humble request."

"Yes?" Rena said, her eyes wet with the seriousness of the exchange.

"In making this deal binding, I ask that you let me spare you the burden of raising your daughter until she is a woman. I will watch over her as if I were her mother—though I am not. I will raise her with love and school her in the ways of Israel, and put her life before mine, if you grant me the right. Do you accept these terms?"

"I *don't*," Rena said. And a terror washed over Yehudit's face. "I will loan you my daughter until she is grown," Rena said, "but only if you both sleep here tonight. No daughter of mine can leave me so sick and head out into such a dark, cold night."

"Of course, of course," Yehudit said, stepping forward. "A deal's a deal." And here, Yehudit hugged Rena, with that burning baby between them—too sick to cry. Into Rena's ear, Yehudit whispered, "Let God protect our husbands in battle. And protect our country at war. Let God save this little daughter, and let God bless this house, and protect you always. And may He bless our new city, though it is now only two hovels on sister hills."

"Amen," Rena said. "Thank you," she said, and kissed her friend on the cheek.

Yehudit stepped back and wiped the tears from her face. "A silly superstition you may think," she said, "but I believe in the power of the word."

Rena looked in the corner at all the milk bottles full of water. "When my boys used to get those terrible fevers, I would give them ice baths to cool them down."

"If I had ice," Yehudit said, "I'd have done it myself."

"There's always a way to make do." Rena took up her gun and walked out to the northern edge of her property, where there was a high boulder that caught the wind. She climbed the boulder in the darkness—already familiar with its every crag. She took up a jerry can she kept there to cool when the temperature dropped, one she'd tuck in the shade each morning, her refreshment as she worked the land. Rena stood on that rock and screwed off the cap. She hoisted the container in the crook of an elbow, looking for any signs of fighting from Jordan. She tipped the can back and took a long swig. And she was comforted as the water sent a chill to her bones.

. . .

When Rena opened her eyes, she found herself in the chair, the gun in her lap, the psalms at her side, and her front door already open, letting in the morning. She went outside and discovered Yehudit sitting under a tree at the western edge of the hill, rocking the baby in her arms, a small machine pistol at her feet. Yehudit turned at Rena's step and smiled up at her friend, and Rena knew from this that the baby had improved in the night.

"Look" is all Yehudit said, pointing out past her own shack on the opposite hill and down into the valley beyond. There, appearing and disappearing, as he blended into the terrain, an Israeli soldier in fatigues made his way toward them, flashing brightest when he unfurled his map and caught the sun.

"A miracle," Rena said.

"A miracle," Yehudit said. Rena first picked up her friend's gun, then thought better about firing off a shot. She went back to the shack and returned with a flare, pulling off its cap, and then jumping and screaming and calling to the soldier. She waved that flare around, throwing it high off the edge of the hill. And he waved.

When the soldier, running double-time, reached the top off the hill, he put his hands to his knees to catch his breath, and then stood, wiping the sweat from his head with an arm.

"A miracle that you should stumble by us," Rena said. "We have a sick baby, and a lady who needs to get to a clinic. Do you have a jeep? She cannot travel this way by foot."

"About a kilometer in from the road. That's as far as I could go before the rise turned too steep."

"Take her," Rena said, giving him a shove. "Hurry down. Who knows how much time is left?"

"I'll take her," the soldier said, tucking his shirt in his pants and his pants in his boots before snapping to attention. "But first," he said, "which one of you is Rena Barak?"

Rena touched the soldier a second time, steadying herself against him. "Then I guess," she said, as Yehudit hurried over to help support her, "that this is no miracle for me."

Rena accepted the news of her husband's death and said, "Thank you, brave soldier. Now find my boys and tell them to bury their father. Their mother waits at home." And here she motioned for Yehudit to start down into the valley, so as not to slow them any further on their way.

"There will be a funeral," the soldier said. "There is room in the jeep for all three."

"Look around you," she said. "Our great settlement is two houses and two families. For both mothers to leave would be to lose everything we've started building. Our neighbors from down the hill will be back up in an instant. And a more unfor-givable sin than never having reclaimed this land would be letting land that is Jewish fall back into Arab hands. Up here, we fight no less of a battle than the one that took my husband. Now tell me, young soldier," Rena said, "how do we fare in this war?"

. . .

There was no mirror in the shack for Rena to cover. The collar of her shirt was already torn. There was hardly a way to harshen her life as an appropriate sign of mourning, and so she sat on the crate that held their books, and she grieved. She spent the next two days perched in the door of their shack, waiting for any traveler who might pass and acknowledge her loss.

On the third day of mourning, Rena was comforted to see her three sons crest the hill. They came carrying supplies on their backs, and with a group of boys in tow.

The sons wept with their mother and then moved aside, so that each of the new boys could approach and welcome Rena into the mourners of Zion.

It was her oldest son, Yermiyahu, who explained things. "These are boys from our yeshiva. They've come to help us make a minyan, so that we can say Kaddish for our father at home."

And it was her second son, Matityahu, who said, baby-faced and trying to appear stoic, "They have taken an oath in honor of our father and his memory."

And the tallest of those boys, momentarily emboldened by the report of his pledge, said, "We make this our home, too. And we will not so much as step off this hill until there are ten for each one of us. Until our seven are seventy."

Her littlest, Tzuki, just past bar mitzvah, came up and hugged her. "Look, Mother, at how our settlement grows."

"Yes, my boy," Rena said, slipping into that space where

every house of mourning for a moment turns happy. "And only weeks ago," she said, tickling at the down of his upper lip, "did we go from having three men to four." All laughed, and then all turned serious as the sons took seats around their mother on the floor. The seven who were not grieving went right to clearing rocks, pulling weeds, and planting their tents on the hill.

II: 1987

It was this day that was talked about for years to come. How sister hills became a city. And so moved were the people who heard the story, they forgot even to ask whatever had happened to the baby girl, and where Hanan was buried, and whether Rena had remarried, and if the Arab boy had ever come back about that tree. They were simply taken with the legend of this sacrifice and the *halutz*-like pioneering commitment of this woman, as well as that of the seven boys who followed her sons back to settle.

The aura of this tale was strengthened by the facts on the ground. One would find it hard to believe that in barely fourteen years, exactly half the life of her youngest, the settlement had grown to such a degree.

There were paved roads, and two schools, and a *kolel*, and a synagogue. And thanks to a Texas evangelist who had fallen in love with that place (before a greater love undid him), their settlement had been gifted with a sports center, complete with the only ice-skating rink in the West Bank as a whole.

It was a city perfectly melded with the contours of the land, circle after circle of houses running down the sides of those hills, and echoing the foregone terraces. There was a perfect symmetry of red roofs and white walls reaching down to the valley floor and edging so close to that Arab village on the eastern side, they'd been forced to take over the village's fields as a security buffer. This gleaming new city was made all the more beautiful by the contrast of those two green hilltops, one with an olive grove and the other bare. The two hilltops belonging to those two founding families looked nearly exactly as they had when those first families returned. All the cement and paved road, all the streetlamps and cobblestones, all the public benches and mailboxes and skinny evergreen trees, all of that came to a stop where the roads wound up to the tops of those hills and came to an end. It was—and the most pious among them couldn't help but say it—like two green teats topping those mountains.

But for the additions of running water and electricity, Rena's shack stayed the same. The only discernible differences to her plot of land were the two-story pole on the southern end, on which sat the siren for announcing war, and, on the northern tip, the stone obelisk that rose from the top of that giant boulder, as if it had somehow forced its way up from within. It was the town's *andarta*. On it were engraved the names of the men of the village who had died at war.

Hanan was the first casualty of those sister hills, and how they'd all wished he'd remained the only name. By the time the intifada was tearing up the West Bank, the list on that stone was too long for a place so young. There was Rena's oldest son, Yermiyahu, killed in Tripoli in '83, as well as two of those pioneering seven boys who'd followed him home, only to die at his side in battle. And, just days before, on the back of a family already saddled with so much tragedy, Rena had lost her second son, her baby-faced Matityahu, now a grown man. He was nearing thirty, and finally engaged to be married that spring. Of course, Matityahu's name had yet to be added to the other eight on that list.

There had been rock-throwing in the Arab village below,

and with a few green soldiers stuck in the wadi beyond and overwhelmed by this kind of close-quarters battle, the men of their town had run down into the fight. And somehow in this melee, Rena had lost a son. Her Mati, her warrior. It wasn't even real warfare, only tear gas and rocks and rubber bullets. Rena still couldn't believe it. A mighty son lost to boys throwing stones.

She was still sitting shiva. And in contrast to when she'd lost her husband and sat three days alone in her doorway like Abraham himself, it was the populace of a small city that now passed through her home. The town had stayed close enough to its roots to revere its founder with something like faith.

The visitor who'd traveled farthest to see her was her youngest, Tzuki, her last living son—though he was already his own kind of casualty to Rena. Tzuki had driven from Haifa, where he lived as a liberal, a secularist, and a gay. He shared an apartment with another boy he'd met at yeshiva. And Tzuki told his mother, with a flash in his eye, that from their balcony they looked upon the water.

To look at her son, as much a founder of their settlement as she was, Rena could not believe how people transform in the span of one life. There he sat, receiving the town with a yarmulke perched on his head, like it was the first he'd ever worn. Where tzitzit would go, a black T-shirt showed through his button-down shirt. And on his arm, exposed for all the world to see, was a tattoo of a dolphin—like the ones that mark the trash who sit and drink beer on the beach in Tel Aviv.

When he'd told her of his lifestyle, she'd sworn never to meet the boy he called his partner. And Tzuki had said that wouldn't be a problem, as he'd sworn never again to cross the Green Line from Israel proper into the territories it held. When his last brother died, she did not think he'd come to see her. And yet, here he was at her side. For this, she put a hand to his hand, and from there they wove fingers. To her son, she said, "It's nice of you to do this for Mati."

"For my brother and for you," he said. Then he stood and joined the men in the grove who'd gathered together to hear him recite the prayer for the dead.

III: 2000

How things change, you wouldn't believe. Another thirteen years pass and those sister hills now cap a metropolis. With the aid of a small bridge of new land, the settlement had merged with a younger community to the west and now looked, on the army maps, like a barbell. And this was exactly the nickname the battalions of Israeli soldiers sent to defend it now used. Along with the new territory came a small religious college that gave out, in handfuls, endless degrees in law. There was a mall with a food court, and a multiplex within it that showed all the American films. There was a boutique hotel and a historical museum and a clinic that could do anything short of transplanting a heart. And along both edges of the connecting roadway between old and new city, there were *dunam* after *dunam* of hydroponic tomatoes set in greenhouses. An operation watered by robot, tended by Thai worker, and whose plants somehow grew with their roots at the top and fat fruit hanging down.

A core group of idealists still remained in that expansive settlement. There were the families of those first seven boys, and the seventy that followed. There were Rav Kook stalwarts, and old-school Messianists, and religious Zionists of every stripe. But this didn't stop the colony's transformation into the bedroom community it had become. Behind the bougainvillea-covered balconies lived professors who drove to Be'er Sheva to teach at the big university, and start-up types who commuted every day to the technical park in Jerusalem, as well as venture capitalists who used Ben Gurion Airport as if it were the Central Bus Station, flying to Europe for a lunch and making it back late the same night. And there was a subset among those new neighbors that the founding residents, the farmers and fighters, could hardly understand: the healthy grown men, pale and soft in the middle, who lived on Japanese and Indian and American clocks, making trades or writing code, supporting large families without ever stepping out into the light.

They came for the tax breaks. They came for the space. They came for the vistas and the fresh air, and because the tomatoes—growing backward, and also without ever seeing sun—still tasted better than anything they'd had in their fancy Orna & Ella salads back on Sheinkin Street.

.   .   .

Though Aheret was a pious girl who wore a skirt to the floor and a shirt that reached to her wrists, she had a worldly allure that belied the choices she'd made. She'd studied at the girls' school on the hill, and done her national service helping the elderly of their town. When the eldest of her younger sisters went off to board in Jerusalem, and when her father was sent by the settler movement to travel across the United States for long stretches to do outreach (his calling) and send home money (a necessity), she'd stayed in the house to help her mother with the littlest of her eight siblings and run their home, a strange maze of additions and tacked-on rooms, that, on the holidays, when all were together, still burst at the seams. These humble choices found Aheret unmarried at twenty-seven, which, in their community, left her seen as an old maid.

When Aheret stepped into the house with a laundry basket full of clean clothes still stiff from the lines, she saw some-one darting around in the back rooms of the house. She at first assumed they were being robbed, until her eyes adjusted to the inside and she made out a silhouette that fit every older woman of their town. *"Gveret!"* she called, not wholly impolitely. "Mis-sus, can I help you? What are you doing in our house?" At that, the woman's ears perked up, and all her nervous energy flooded out toward Aheret, with the woman, riding it like a wave, right behind.

"Your mother," the woman called. "Where's your mother?" she said.

"Hanging what's wet," Aheret said, and pointed through the wall to the lines.

"Come, come," the woman said, grabbing Aheret's arm, sometimes leading, sometimes following, as they both rushed around the house.

With a clothespin in her mouth and a wet sock in her hand, Yehudit looked at the pair hurrying toward her and tilted her head to the side.

"Is this the one I bought?" Rena yelled, pulling Aheret. "Is this the one that's mine?"

And Aheret, who had never been told the story of her near death, was more surprised by her mother's answer than by the question of the lady who pulled her. For Yehudit dropped the sock into the basket and pulled the clothespin from her lips and said, "Yes, yes. This is the one that's yours."

. . .

Despite the fact that the hilltops were forever facing, the difference between the two families' lives and the two families' fates had put far more distance than the geography in between. To anyone who still knew she was up there, Rena was simply the old woman in the olive grove, while Yehudit, with her brood, took advantage of the settlement's great blooming and lived a vibrant life.

Yehudit had not forgotten her sister founder, who, despite her great sacrifice, had been dealt a harsh life. She'd gone over every few months to check on Rena, and Yehudit always acted surprised to discover that she carried with her a cake or a cooked chicken in the bag in her hand. As loyal as she was to Rena, she could tell that all her troubles had turned the woman hard. And though Yehudit took her children to visit other lonely souls, it had been a very long time since she'd taken any of them up to visit Rena in the grove. Because of this, Rena hadn't set eyes on Yehudit's daughter in years, and the same went for Aheret in relation to the woman she knew from her mother as Mrs. Barak.

Rena had let go of Aheret's arm to pull a little Nokia phone from the pocket of her skirt. It was a phone no different from the other million phones the supermarkets had given away when the cell towers went up. She held this out to Yehudit and her daughter, as if looking at it alone would let them read the calls inside.

"Tzuki," she said. "My last boy has been killed."

Yehudit and Aheret, like every citizen of that country, were up-to-date on the national news of the day. There'd been nothing in Lebanon or Gaza, no terrorist attack listed on the radio at the top of the hour. It was a quiet September morning.

But it wasn't any outside force, not politics, or religion, that did Tzuki in. It was Israel's own internal plague that had taken him, the one that took more children of Israel than all the bloodshed and hatred of all their long wars combined. "Hit," Rena said. "The coastal highway. Run off the road by a boy driving one hundred and eighty kilometers an hour."

"*Baruch dayan emet,*" Aheret said. And then: "Mercy upon you, a terrible loss."

"Sit, sit," Yehudit said, overturning the basket of clean laundry and helping Rena to sit down. "Another tragedy," she said. "How many can fall on one home?" As she said this, she stepped over to the eaves and began tearing wildly at a little mint plant, one among many at the side of the house. She held these leaves out to Aheret, letting them fall in wet clumps into her daughter's hands. "Go," she said, "make Rena a hot cup of tea."

Before Aheret ran off, Rena had ahold of her skirt. "No need for tea," she said to Yehudit. "We're not staying long."

And here, Aheret, who did not know the story of her childhood sickness, who did not know of the deal that had been struck, reflected on this statement along with the exchange she'd heard earlier.

Growing up, Aheret would lie with her head in her mother's lap and beg her to run her fingers through her hair, and to tell the stories that came before remembering. The one Yehudit always told with great pride was that once upon a time, there were in this place two empty mountains that God had long ago given Israel but that Israel had long forgotten. And one day, two brave families had come to settle those mountains. The first had three young boys, and the other came up that hill alone and bore a baby girl who was, for the future of their settlement, as great a gift as Adam's finding Eve.

Aheret now stared at her mother, and knew from her face that there was another story she'd not been told.

"Look this way," Rena said, pulling at that skirt, drawing Aheret's eyes to her. "Look to me, at *this* face. Here is where your questions now go."

Rena then pulled hard at the skirt, not to draw Aheret

down, but to pull herself up. Standing, staring at Aheret, she said, "Come along."

"Please," Yehudit said. "You can't really want it this way? Today—despite your sadness—is not really any different. Tzuki, before this accident, was already, to you, long gone."

"A child distant," Rena said, "a child rebellious, a child cut off in head and heart, it is not the same as no child at all. You have always been a smart woman," Rena said. "And what takes place here is not remotely equal. But in a moment, you'll have the first tiny inkling of how I three times over feel."

"It was a joke," Yehudit said, panicked and referring back to their deal. "The whole thing a silly superstition. You said yourself—almost thirty years ago, and I remember like yesterday—you said it was just old-country mumbo jumbo, a worried mother's game."

"A deal is a deal," Rena said to Yehudit. And to Aheret, she said, "Daughter, come along."

. . .

The woman had just buried her last son. The woman gone mad. And Yehudit, who had been through it all with her, who had built this giant city at her side, thought it would not hurt to send her daughter to walk the woman back, to help her into her mourning, to stay and offer comfort and maybe cook for her a meal. Think about it. A husband killed at the start of her new life. Two sons cut down as heroes and a third, already lost to her, run off the side of the road. And here was Yehudit, blessed with nine, all healthy and happy, and with a husband she loved who was often far from her side but who sent back Jew after Jew in his stead. Benevolent, Yehudit sent Aheret with her. And Aheret, only half filled in on the story and half comprehending, was a dutiful daughter and understood the strange favors that sometimes fell to a neighbor when someone was in pain.

As the pair started to walk down the hill, Aheret turned back toward her mother, hoping for a signal, trying to communicate while maintaining respect under this watchful woman's eye. And Rena said, "I can see the question you are trying to ask, daughter. The answer is simple. You were sold to me as a child. And, for all intents and purposes, you are mine."

"Mother!" Aheret called to Yehudit, unable to contain herself.

But it was Rena, again holding her skirt, who gave the girl a yank and said, "What?"

. . .

"It is the madness of grief," the rabbi said as Yehudit trailed after him in the supermarket. She'd tracked him down, first by calling the shul, and then the *kolel,* and then the school, where his secretary said he'd run out to the supermarket for supplies. That's where Yehudit found him, pushing a cart tumbled full with cartons of ice cream, a treat to the students for some charitable act. He'd said, "We do the right thing because it is right— that doesn't mean a child can't be rewarded just the same." As for the story he was hearing, he said, "When the shiva is over, I can promise you, *bli neder,* that Mrs. Barak won't want to treat such a trivial pledge as a binding contract at all."

Yehudit stood there in the freezer aisle and looked as if she was going to weep. The rabbi nodded in the way thoughtful rabbis do. He was a tall man, and slim, and even into his later years his beard had stayed black. He looked twenty years younger than he was, and so when he smiled at her kindly, there was a separate sort of calm that Yehudit felt, a husbandly calm, which was very fulfilling in the moment, with her own husband so far away.

"I know you don't want to say it," the rabbi said, "but it is not *lashon hara* to point out between us that you're afraid Rena's heart has hardened over all these lonely years."

"That is what I fear," Yehudit said.

"Then let me pose for you a scenario of a different sort. Even if she takes you to rabbinical court, and you face the *beit din* over this case, can you imagine such a thing holding up?" When she did not answer, he said it again. "Well, can you imagine me taking her side?"

"No," Yehudit said.

"So let us remember that without that woman, as much as without you, the great miracle that is our lives in this place would not be. And even if she'd contributed nothing to its founding, even if—God forbid—she had only taken, and done harm, still, can we not pity her in this time of grief? Especially a woman who has known sadness so much more than joy?"

"Yes," Yehudit said. Though the question was not wiped from her face.

"Go on," he said, "what is it?"

"Can you tell me, Rebbe—and I understand the word— but what, with my daughter taken, does *pity* mean?"

"It means would it hurt Aheret to stay by this woman's side through to the end of the period of mourning?"

Yehudit went to answer, and the rabbi raised a silencing hand. "After their ice cream, I will send up the boys to pray. I will send up some girls to help. Your daughter will not be left alone. And if harboring such a fantasy allows Rena to survive this week, how bad is it to indulge for a little while?"

"And what if she doesn't give it up?"

"Then you will convene a rabbinical court, over which I myself will preside. And I promise you, even if it's an hour before Shabbat that you come to me, I will find another two *rabbanim,* and we'll settle the matter right then. But I will not bring one of the two mothers of this community, who has just lost her last son, to stand in judgment today."

"All right," Yehudit said. "If Aheret is willing, I will let her stay until Rena rises from mourning."

.   .   .

The period of shiva was not like it was for Mati, and not like it was for Yermiyahu. It better resembled how it had been when she'd lost her husband, Hanan. The new people of the city did not know Rena. And the staunch Mizrahi religious had forgotten her son when she herself had cut him off. Many others in town, though they did not say it, felt the boy had been punished for his evil ways, and they worried that, in visiting his mother, such a thought might show up in their eyes. So they made themselves busy with other things, and they told themselves they would visit on another day, until all the days were done.

Once again, the minyan at Rena's shack was comprised of volunteer boys sent from a yeshiva down the hill. The main difference was that the girls were sent along with them to try to cheer her, and, of course, there was Aheret, taking care.

When Rena addressed Aheret, she'd say, "Daughter, some tea," or "Daughter, a biscuit." And those bright student girls who sat with Rena could not understand why this woman grieved for her son but her daughter did not cry over her brother. To them, Rena would say, "A very long story, how I alone sit shiva and the sister does not mourn."

For Aheret, sleeping on a cot in that one-room shack, her only peace was on her nightly walk to the outdoor bathroom. Plumbed though it was, it was separate from the house. On her way, Aheret would sneak over to the boulder on which the memorial obelisk stood. She would read the names of the town's fallen by flashlight and understand that her sacrifice was small.

Yehudit came every day to pay her respects, and to see that the girl who had been her daughter was well. She took it upon herself to bake a simple cake for the final service of the shiva, so that she would be there when the bereaved stood up from mourning and first exited the house.

Poised in the sun with Aheret at her side, Yehudit watched in silence as Rena circled the top of the hill, enacting the traditional walk that marked the week's close. When Rena arrived at the door once again, Yehudit wished her a long and healthy life, then took Aheret's hand and said, "Come, my child, let's go."

Rena tilted her head, quizzical, just as Yehudit had when Rena came around the house, dragging Aheret her way. "Where do you take my daughter?" Rena said. "The end of the week does not end the bond."

Yehudit had planned for this moment, rehearsing it ceaselessly in her head. She pulled from her pocket the original bill with which Rena had paid her. She'd saved it as a keepsake all these years.

Rena laughed. *"Lirot?"* she said. "Not even valid currency anymore."

"Then I'll pay in shekels, or dollars. You name your price."

"A price on a girl like this?" Rena said. "What kind of mother would sell her daughter?"

"You know why I did it," Yehudit said. "To save her."

"I also know when you did it. And I know what has changed." Rena signaled all that was around them. "What did we pay for these hills so many years before? Now think of what it would cost to buy the city that sits atop them. Understand, Yehudit—I'm alone in the world but for my daughter. For all the riches this world contains, I wouldn't sell her away. She is my peace, and my comfort"—and here Rena stepped over and put a delicate touch on Aheret's cheek, "my life."

Then Rena's touch changed, and she circled that hand around Aheret's wrist, holding tight.

"Mother," Aheret called, now truly frightened.

And again, it was Rena who answered the call.

.   .   .

Three rabbis sat under the shade of the giant olive tree. They were perched on molded plastic chairs, a plastic table before them. Rena had defied their order to appear in their court, on the grounds that a case so obvious was no case at all. And when Rabbi Kiggel (the man with the ice cream) offered to bring the panel of judges to her, Rena said only, "My door has been open to all comers since before there was anyone to come."

And so the rabbis drove up to where the road ends, the plastic furniture tied to the roof of their Subaru, and they took their places under the tree that would offer the most shade. Since none of the rabbis knew to look, they did not notice the scar at the tree's base, grown over in keloid fashion, and healed up in the interim twenty-seven years.

Across from the rabbis stood Aheret and her mother, Yehudit. And in a chair carried from the house, Aheret's other mother, Rena, sat facing the rabbis, waiting for her turn to speak. Yehudit spoke passionately and with great urgency, and Rena did not listen. She just stared at the two rabbis flanking Kiggel's side. If Kiggel was ten years older than Rena, then the one to his right was another ten years older than that. As for the child rabbi to his left, Rena didn't believe he'd yet been bar mitzvahed. Before he'd been allowed to sit in judgment of her, she'd have preferred if they'd pulled down his pants to make sure that, at the very least, he had his three hairs.

When Yehudit was done, she again presented the single bill with which Rena had purchased her daughter. This, the rabbis placed on their table, under the weight of a stone.

"A boy" is what Rena said, pointing at the young rabbi. "A child who has never known a world with a divided Jerusalem. Who was raised in a greater Israel, where he can pray at the foot of our Holy Temple in a united city, where he can cross the Jordan without fear and stare down at his country from atop the Golan Heights. And here he sits in judgment on my land, in the heart of Samaria, because of the sacrifices made before he was born."

Kiggel went to speak, but it was the young rabbi who put a hand to his arm to answer on his own.

"This I acknowledge," the boy rabbi said. "But in this life, I've already achieved—and this court would appreciate the respect it is due."

"And what respect is that?" Rena said.

"The respect that comes with law. You have sacrificed," he said. "You have fought. And I continue the fight my own way. Look at us. We live in a Jewish country, with a Jewish government, and yet its false, secular courts send Jewish soldiers to knock down the houses we build. They arrest our brothers as vigilantes, who only protect what God has given. And those same judges, in those same courts, give Arabs the rights of Jews—as if a passport is all it takes to make a person a citizen of this land. You fought your battles, and now we fight ours. I am thankful there are avenues in this country where one may be judged by Jewish law, as the Holy One—blessed is He—intended."

"You will judge me as God intended?"

"We will judge based on the law that is within the grasp of humble man."

"That is all I wanted to hear." And Rena stood up from her chair. She approached the three rabbis. She looked to Yehudit and to Aheret, her daughter.

"It is not far from here," Rena said, "where Esav returned from the hunt, tired and hungry, and traded away his birthright for a bowl of red lentils. It is among these very hills where Abraham, our father, took a heifer, three years old, and a goat, three years old, and a ram, three years old, and a turtledove, three years old, and a young pigeon and split them all, but for those birds, and left them for the vultures in a covenant with God, which gives us the right to this land as a whole. And for four hundred shekels of silver, Abraham bought the cave in which he lies buried—and over which, with our Arab neighbors, we spill blood until this very day. So tell me, these contracts, with God and man, written down nowhere, only remembered, do they still hold?"

And the rabbis looked at one another, and the ancient rabbi on the right, the white of the beard around his mouth stained brown, said, "Do not turn this day into one of blasphemy. Do not dare compare our modern trivialities to what was done in biblical times."

"I ask only does the verbal contract with which God granted us this nation stand, or does it not? With respect, with honor, I ask."

"We do not need a paper when the contracts are with God. And the ones you list that are between man and man—those, too, are recorded in the Torah, which is also, every word and every letter, whispered by God into Moses' ear. The answer is, they are valid, and unquestionable, and, also, do not compare."

It was Kiggel who then spoke. "I ask you, Gveret Barak.

I know you do not intend blasphemy, I know this matter is charged. But let us use perspective. Let us keep things in their right size."

It was Yehudit who screamed at this, "My daughter, my daughter's life—do not treat it as small."

"*My* daughter," Rena said, correcting her. "My daughter, as much as this is my city, as much as this court convenes at my home. If you want to reject our ancient covenants as irrelevant, then let us talk about modern times. From the very first day Yehudit and her husband bought their hill, and my husband and I purchased the one on which you sit, the Arabs in the village right there below have claimed it a false contract, a purchase made from a relative who had no right to sell."

"This is the Arab way," Rabbi Kiggel said.

"Well, is our city built on a lie? It is not three thousand years old, but thirty. If they claim their contract false—a contract entered into the same year as the one now in dispute—do we give up our homes? Do we give up our city? For they, too— like the bill that flutters on your table—are willing to pay back the amount they received."

"A Jewish court," the young rabbi said. "It is not the same what happens between the Jew and the Gentile. And it is not the same what happens between peoples at war."

Rena looked to Yehudit and Aheret and then to the rabbis before her.

"I see," she said. "This is a false court. You try to trick an old woman in mourning, a lonely woman. Judgment has already been passed, hasn't it? There is no way I can win."

"No," Kiggel said, "you will be awarded motherhood, if you are right."

"Promise it," Rena said. And pointing to Yehudit and Aheret, she said, "Make them both promise that they will follow what this *beit din* decides. I will not have this settled by emotion. If it is a valid court, and an honest court, I will have it settled by what is right."

"You will," Kiggel said.

"We will follow the court's ruling," Yehudit said.

"From her," Rena said, pointing at the girl. "From her I want to hear it."

"I am a founder of this city," Aheret said, "the same as you two, only more. I was born to these hills and to these hills I will return. I know no other place. And no other world. If this is what the rabbis decide, if this is the law of the land, then so be it. My life, it's in God's hands. I will follow the ruling of this court."

"Tomorrow is Rosh Hashanah," Rena said. And Yehudit blanched at the news. When, in her life, had a holiday been forgotten? Her children would all be home; she'd need to start her cooking. And then she wondered if, at her table, she'd have eight or nine. "From tomorrow, we move into the Ten Days of Repentance, when God decides who will live and who will die. Let each of you pledge to judge honestly, or be written out of the Book of Life. Then I, too—I promise—will accept whatever it is you say."

The rabbis conferred among themselves. They were going to judge honestly. They were honest men. But to take an unnecessary pledge set a dangerous precedent. It was not to be done lightly—and not an easy thing on which to agree.

"We'd prefer to avoid that kind of extremism," Kiggel said to Rena.

"Then you do not have my trust."

Again they conferred, and finally they consented, and the young rabbi said, "We will judge honestly, or let us be written out of the Book of Life."

"Then I need raise only one simple point," Rena said, "and the case will be resolved."

The rabbis nodded, allowing it.

"If you three pious men will grant me that you are kosher, then you will also grant that the girl is mine."

"One," Kiggel said, "does not follow the other."

"But it does," she said. "You're going to side against me because my contract with Yehudit, you will say, is symbolic. Because my contract with Yehudit can't be considered to be a contract at all."

"I don't want to say one way or the other," Kiggel said, "but there are many facts that lead a logical person this way."

"So, I ask you, once again, are the three of you kosher? Have you knowingly broken the rules of what is fit to eat?"

"We have not knowingly done so," the young rabbi said.

"Tomorrow is Rosh Hashanah," Rena said. "Do the three of you observe the Jewish holidays? Are you faithful in carrying out Jewish law?"

Once again the young rabbi answered, saying, "It is safe to assume."

"Then tell me," Rena said, "if you are willing to state that my deed on this land is sound, and ignore the Arab claims against it, if you are willing to accept biblical contracts as eternally valid, though we have no proof beyond faith that they ever were, I ask you, very simply, every year, on Passover, when you sell your *hametz* to a Gentile so as not to break the edict of having any trace of it under your roof, when everyone in your congregations comes to you and says, 'Rabbi, for this week when it's prohibited for a Jew to have even one crumb of bread in his house, sell all that is forbidden to a Gentile so that we may inhabit our homes,' is that contract real?"

"This is the tradition," the young rabbi said. "And that contract is as legal as any other."

"And in all your years, have you ever heard of a single Gentile anywhere in the world stepping into a Jewish home to open a cabinet and take what is rightfully his? Is there known to you such a case?"

The rabbis looked at one another, and their answer was no.

"So tell me, if the selling of the *hametz* is based on a contract that's never once been exercised in all the years of your lives in all the world over, can you still say that it is a valid contract in your eyes? Or do you admit that, really, each one of us—each one of you!—is in possession of *hametz* every Passover, and that no Jew really observes the holiday as commanded?"

"God forbid!" the rabbis said, all three.

Then the old rabbi said, "You find yourself on the edge of blasphemy once again. But if there is a point to be made, then, yes, that contract is valid, exercised or no."

"If that contract is valid, if you three can still call yourselves kosher, then you have to admit, equally valid is mine. Just because it's assumed that one party will never exercise her rights doesn't mean the rights are not hers."

And here the rabbis whispered, and all three took out their pens and began passing one another notes, looking terribly concerned. For a judge can know how his heart would decide, but his obligation is always to the law. And they had sworn, these three. Sworn on their lives. A terrible promise to make.

"And tell me this," Rena said. "When a little bar mitzvah boy says to a pretty girl as a joke, 'You are my wife,' and he gives her a bracelet as a token—"

"A divorce is arranged," the young rabbi said. "We have done it before. Yes, if it is uttered and the gift received, they are married, the same as any two people in the world."

"Even if neither really meant it?" Rena said. "Even if an innocent joke between two young adults at play?"

"Even then," said Rabbi Kiggel.

"That is all I'm saying," Rena said. "That a contract

doesn't require either party to intend to exercise its terms, or even for both parties to be mature enough to grasp them. And likewise a symbolic contract, like that of Passover, whose intent at signing is that it would never be put into use, is as valid as any other in the eyes of God. So all you're really deciding in this case is if the money on the table before you was of any value at the time the deal was made. That is all the court is being asked. If you are religious men, following religious law, then there is nothing to say but that the girl belongs to me."

"The same as a slave, though," Kiggel said, a finger raised. "That's how it would be."

"Call it what you will, but the girl is mine."

.   .   .

Aheret stood in the dark on the western edge of the hill. Rosh Hashanah dinner had finished. And she'd come out to the edge of the grove to stare across to the hill opposite, where she could see that her mother had left a light burning in the window so Aheret would know that she was not forgotten.

It was the second night since the verdict, and so different from those first days when she'd tended to this woman during her week of mourning. Aheret was hopeless, and—since suicide was forbidden, a grave sin—she could only wish and pray that the world, for her, would come to an end. Let me be left out of the Book of Life, she thought. Let my fate be decided this week. Let the sky up above come crashing down.

And it was, right then, as if Aheret's prayers were answered.

Though it was not the sky that was falling, but the earth shaking as if it planned to swallow up the whole hill. There was nothing to see from the side of the summit on which Aheret stood. No dust rose up in the distance, as when Hanan had caught the armored corps rolling down toward the Yom Kippur War.

It was from the other side of the little shack that the sound of great conflagration came, and anyone who hadn't been raised on those hills might have thought they were already surrounded. It took a lifetime to learn how the specific echoes bounced off the range.

Aheret hadn't wanted to stand on that side of the house ever again. That's where her fate had been sealed. Where her two mothers had stood silent before the rabbis, as stiff as the trees around them, as abiding as the sister hills themselves.

What she saw when she rounded the house and passed the big tree and stood at the edge was a battle being raged inside Israel like none she had ever seen. The village below was practically afire, not with the force of Israeli aggression, but with the unleashing of a new kind of Palestinian rage. The bypass roads that had sprung up throughout her lifetime were blocked, tires burning at every edge. There was the sound of light arms, at first intermittent and then turning frequent as more Arabs than she ever knew existed streamed out to fight the Israeli soldiers who'd already arrived. In the sky, coming from Jerusalem, she could see the lights of the Black Hawks and Cobras as the helicopters raced their way. And then she saw nothing as the helicopters went dark so as to enter the fight in stealth. Of all the ends to this country she'd imagined, this was not one foreseen. She did not think, since the time of its founding, that it had ever known such violence to rise up within its borders.

That is when she noticed Rena at her side, handing her an Uzi to match her own.

"Do you think," Aheret said, "the whole country is like this?"

"It's another intifada," Rena said. "Look," she added, pointing to a vehicle of the Palestinian Authority. "Which naïve Jew thought it was safe to give them guns? And on a holy day again they attack." Rena turned toward the tree and looked down at the battle truly raging below. She said, "Tonight it comes down. We can never let ourselves be sneaked up on again."

Rena rushed back to the shack. And, wearing her festival dress, she returned with an ax in hand.

"It is *yom tov* tonight," Aheret said. "Forbidden."

"In an emergency such measures are allowed." She handed the ax to her daughter, who did not take it from her.

"I won't," Aheret said. "The soldiers fight. The Arabs do not yet come up the hill. And still, if the war shifts this way, seeing it overtake us from the window won't help us to survive."

"Insolent daughter," Rena said. "I'll do it myself." And Rena pulled up her sleeves, and she hacked and hacked at that tree. Rena chopped for hours, and no one heard a single blow echo off the mountains, drowned out as they were by the fight.

This time, Rena did not stop because she was tired. She did not stop because her arms were weak. She would not let age get in her way, or the pains of her body, or the shortness of breath. She did not even heed Aheret's calls from the shack when the girl told her it was too much and to quit for the night. Rena did not stop until that tree was felled. And it was the sound of it hitting that sent Aheret back outside in the morning light.

What the girl found was the tree fallen over, and Rena fallen at its side. Her mother held the ax in one hand, and the other reached across her chest, grabbing at that ax-holding arm. Rena's face had gone slack, a racking pain clearly troubling one side. And Aheret could see on this woman—who'd aged a hundred years in a night, and breathed in the most labored fashion—a terror in her eyes.

Aheret took mercy. She leaned down to count out Rena's

pulse. She had, as said, done her national service with the aged on those two hills, and was well versed in the maladies that struck its residents with time.

"Am I dying?" Rena said.

Aheret thought about this. And the honest answer—she would bet on it—was the one she gave: "No. No, you are not."

"Call the ambulance," Rena said.

"Yes," Aheret said, but it was not the *Yes* of affirmation, but of considered thought. Aheret was consumed with the question of Rena's current state and how it compared with her own. "I will call, Mother, absolutely. But the issue at hand is, when? It is—you are right—permissible to pick up a phone on a holy day if it is a life-and-death situation. But the fact that you are still with us may mean the danger has already passed."

"I think," Rena said, "a heart attack."

And Aheret said, "I think you are right. But if it was big enough to be fatal, I'm fairly sure you'd already be dead. What is at stake now, my guess, from my limited knowledge, is the extent of the recovery you may expect. That is where speed is of the essence."

"What do you say, daughter?" Rena said, looking panicked and confused in the dirt.

"I'd imagine, if we get you help in a hurry, you'll be fine altogether once again. You will be your old self. This is not a question of life and death; what it is, is a question of life and quality of life. If I leave you here by your tree until the end of the holiday, if I wait until it's permissible to use a phone, I can't say that things will turn out well at all. If you think you are weak now, Mother, if you think you are in pain, then understand, just lifting a glass to your mouth for a sip of water will feel like carrying this mountain on your back. I have seen the old people with damaged hearts and soggy lungs. It is not a life to be lived."

"A commandment," Rena said. "To honor your parents. You must."

"Not when your parent tells you to break a holy law."

"Permissible! No matter what." And again Rena puffed out a feeble "Life and death."

"But you are still living, with all these minutes ticked by. No, I really don't see it as such. We will ask those three wise rabbis to convene after the holiday and decide, and they will tell us if, by law, I did what's right."

"Cursed girl," Rena said.

"What you mean is 'cursed daughter.' Not long under this roof and already I learn from you how to get my way. Never in that other house would such a thought have been born. Now listen close, it's very simple: If you free me, I will call right now. I will see you to the hospital and I will—on my word—tend to you until you are back up on your feet. I will do it, not as your daughter, but as a daughter of Israel and of this settlement. I will treat you as I would have before you ever cashed in your bond. Free me, and I call. Free me, and there is a great chance you will be able to walk again, and live again, and return to a normal life. Free me, and you'll be able to dress yourself, and walk yourself, and enjoy what years you have left. Don't you want that? A trade? Your freedom for mine."

"Don't need it," she said, breathing out short and heavy. "Don't need to take care, don't need to walk."

"How can you say that?" Aheret yelled.

"Because I have you to take care."

IV: 2011

Dmitry and Lisa stand on the edge of the hill and stare at an endless stretch of security wall. "Most of it's just fence in these parts" is what their real estate agent says, "but here, because the village is so close and because the fighting back at the start was so fierce, they've got a good rebar concrete wall running the whole way. You can't do any better when it comes to security than that. And no need even to think about it. Really, put it out of your mind. This stretch has been quiet for going on ten years. Still, no one should be unwary in these parts. God forbid something were ever to start up—look, no direct line of fire, no sniper trouble, no hiding under your bed. Intifada Three starts, and I promise you, it won't make a peep in your life."

"And Internet," Dmitry says. "Out here in the boondocks, is the building wired for high speed?"

"Every unit," the agent says, "and over there," he says, pointing to the obelisk on the giant boulder at the edge of the hill, "hidden behind it are signal boosters, so even if you don't get your own router, the whole town, free Wi-Fi, and the best cell-phone service between here and Dubai. Do you want to see upstairs?"

"Let's see upstairs," Lisa says, and then apologizes for her accent. "You'd never believe," she says, "that the two of us fell in love in the same *ulpan* class—his Hebrew so much better than mine."

"The Russians learn quick," the real estate agent says, smiling at Dmitry. And Dmitry smiles a strained smile in return.

On the way into the apartment building, Lisa looks back at the wall. "I mean, are they okay?" she says. "Do they treat the Palestinians all right on the other side of the wall? We are kind of left-wing, you know. I mean, for the space, we'll live here, for the extra bedrooms, but, you know, we feel bad for the Arabs, with all the roadblocks and things like that."

Now Dmitry smiles a real smile. "She doesn't want to live among radicals," he says. "She's from Cherry Hill, in America. They worry about equal everything over there."

"'Radicals'?" the real estate agent says, completely surprised by the notion. "No, always this place, since the seventies, this town has gotten along with its neighbors. Always friendly relations, and attending one another's weddings. It was all very close over here until the First Intifada broke out. Until then, where one place ended and the other started, who knew?"

"Because we don't want the politics," Lisa says. "I mean the building is beautiful, and the area—it's just stunning. But we're not settlers. And we don't want to be surrounded by that sort."

Here the real estate agent walks them through what could be their new kitchen, and what could be their new living room, and presses the button that raises the automatic security shade. He leads them out onto what could be their new balcony, all the while continuing to talk.

"If you mean those crazy Levinger-type settlers, then not at all," he says directly to Lisa, who listens. The words glance off Dmitry, who takes an owner's stance, leaning on the bar of the balustrade and staring out, pretending that it's already his view. "Are there stubborn people here?" the real estate agent asks. "Sure! There are plenty of stubborn—like with all good Israelis." He points to a little shack beneath the balcony, around which the building's carports were built. "The old woman there," he says, and Lisa and Dmitry follow his finger, "she needed the money for selling the land, but she wouldn't, for any amount, let the developer buy her out. There is that kind of steadfastness. And where do you get that from but the real salt of the earth?" As if to demonstrate his point, rolling down a ramp out of the shack's front door comes a wheelchair with an old woman in it, and pushed by a drawn middle-aged woman behind.

"Do you see?" the real estate agent says. "Sweet as sugar. Those are the kind of people that founded this place. That's who the old-type neighbors will be. A sick elderly mother, and a daughter who gives over her life to care for her. Every time I'm here, I see that pair rolling around, just minding their own business. You two will be happy here," he says, "I promise. This is the kind of hill on which to make a life."

How We Avenged
the Blums

If you head out to Greenheath, Long Island, today, you'll find that the school yard where Zvi Blum was attacked is more or less as it was. The bell at the public school still rings through the weekend, and the bushes behind the lot where we played hockey still stand. The only difference is that the sharp screws and jagged edges of the jungle gym are gone, the playground stripped of all adventure, sissified and padded and covered with a snow of shredded tires.

It was onto this lot that Zvi Blum, the littlest of the three Blum boys, stepped. During the week we played in the parking lot of our yeshiva, where slap shots sent gravel flying, but on Shabbos afternoons we ventured onto the fine, uncracked asphalt at the public school. The first to arrive for our game, Zvi wore his helmet with the metal face protector snapped in place. He had on his gloves, and held a stick in his hand.

Zvi worked up a sweat playing a fantasy game while he waited for the rest of us to arrive. After a fake around an imaginary opponent, he found himself at a real and sudden halt. The boy we feared most stood before him. It was Greenheath's local anti-Semite, with a row of friends beyond. The Anti-Semite had, until then, abided by a certain understanding. We stepped gingerly in his presence, looking beaten, which seemed to satisfy his need to beat us for real.

The Anti-Semite took hold of Zvi's face mask as if little Blum were a bowling ball.

Zvi looked past the bully and the jungle gym, through the chain-link fence, and up Crocus Avenue, hoping we'd appear, a dozen or more boys, wearing helmets, wielding sticks. How nice if, like an army, we'd arrived.

The Anti-Semite let go of Zvi's mask.

"You Jewish?" he asked.

"I don't know," Zvi said.

"You don't know if you're Jewish?"

"No," Zvi said. He scratched at the asphalt with his hockey stick.

The bully turned to his friends, taking a poll of suspicious glances.

"Your mother never told you?" the Anti-Semite asked.

Zvi shifted his weight and kept on with his scratching. "It never came up," he said.

Zvi remembered a distinct extended pause while the Anti-Semite considered. Zvi thought—he may have been wishing—that he saw the first of us coming down the road.

He was out cold when we got there, beaten unconscious with his helmet on, his stick and gloves missing. We were no experts at forensics, but we knew immediately that he'd been worsted. And because he was suspended by his underwear from one of the bolts on the swing set, we also knew that a wedgie had been administered along the way.

We thought he was dead.

We had no dimes even to make a telephone call, money being forbidden on the Sabbath. We did nothing for way too long. Then Beryl started crying, and Harry ran to the Vilmsteins, who debated, while they fetched the *mukzeh* keys, which of them should drive in an emergency.

. . .

Some whispered that our nemesis was half Jewish. His house was nestled in the dead end behind our school. And the ire of the Anti-Semite and his family was said to have been awakened when, after he'd attended kindergarten with us at our yeshiva for some months, and had been welcomed as a little son of Israel, the rabbis discovered that only his father was Jewish. The boy, deemed Gentile, was ejected from the class and led home by his shamefaced mother. Rabbi Federbush latched the back gate behind them as the boy licked at the finger paint, nontoxic and still wet on his hands.

We all knew the story, and I wondered what it was like for that boy, growing up—growing large—on the other side of the fence. His mother sometimes looked our way as she came and went from the house. She didn't reveal anything that we were mature enough to read—only kept on, often with a palm pressed to the small of her back.

. . .

After Zvi's beating, the police were called.

My parents wouldn't have done it, and let that fact be known.

"What good will come?" my father said. Zvi's parents had already determined that their son had suffered nothing beyond bruising: his bones were unbroken and his brain unconcussed.

"Call the police on every anti-Semite," my mother said, "and they'll need a separate force." The Blums thought differently. Mrs. Blum's parents had been born in America. She had grown up in Connecticut and attended public school. She felt no distrust for the uniform, believed the authorities were there to protect her.

The police cruiser rolled slowly down the hill with the Blums in procession behind it. They marched, the parents and three sons, little Zvi with his gauze-wrapped head held high.

The police spoke to the Anti-Semite's mother, who propped the screen door open with a foot. After her son had been called to the door for questioning, Mrs. Blum and Zvi were waved up. They approached, but did not touch, the three brick steps.

It was word against word. An accusing mother and son, a pair disputing, and no witnesses to be had. The police didn't make an arrest, and the Blums did not press charges. The retribution exacted from the Anti-Semite that day came in the form of a motherly chiding.

The boy's mother looked at the police, at the Blums, and at the three steps between them. She took her boy by the collar and, pulling him down to a manageable height, slapped him across the face.

"Whether it's niggers or kids with horns," she said, "I don't want you beating on those that are small."

. . .

We'd long imagined that Greenheath was like any other town, except for its concentration of girls in ankle-length jean skirts and white canvas Keds, and boys in sloppy oxford shirts, with their yarmulkes hanging down as if sewn to the side of their heads. There was the fathers' weekday ritual. When they disembarked from the cars of the Long Island Railroad in the evenings, hands reached into pockets and yarmulkes were slipped back in place. The beating reminded us that these differences were not so small.

Our parents were born and raised in Brooklyn. In Green-heath, they built us a Jewish Shangri-la, providing us with everything but the one crucial thing Brooklyn had offered. It wasn't stickball or kick the can—acceptable losses, though nostalgia ran high. No, it was a *quality* that we were missing, a toughness. As a group of boys thirteen and fourteen, we grew healthy, we grew polite, but our parents thought us soft.

Frightened as we were, we thought so, too, which is why we turned to Ace Cohen. He was the biggest Jew in town, and our senior by half a dozen years. He was the toughest Jew we knew, the only one who smoked pot, who had ever been arrested, and who owned both a broken motorcycle and an arcade version of Asteroids. He left the coin panel open and would play endlessly on a single quarter, fishing it out when he was finished. In our admiration, we never considered that at nineteen or twenty we might want to move out of our parents' basements, or go to college. We thought only that he lived the good life—no cares, no job, his own Asteroids, and a minifridge by his bed where he kept his Ring Dings ice-cold.

"Not my beef, little Jew boys" is what he told us when we begged him to beat up the Anti-Semite on our behalf. "Violence breeds violence," he said, slapping at buttons. "Older and wiser—trust me when I tell you to let it go."

"We called the police," Zvi said. "We went to his house with my parents and them."

"Unfortunate," Ace said, looking down at little Zvi. "Unfortunate, my buddy, for you."

"It's a delicate thing being Jewish," Ace said. "It's a condition that aggravates the more mind you pay it. Let it go, I tell you. If you insist on fighting, then at least fight him yourselves."

"It would be easier if you did," we told him.

"And I bet, big as your anti-Semite is, that he, too, in direct proportion, also has bigger friends. Escalation," Ace said.

"Escalation built in. You don't want this to get so bad that you really need me."

"But what if we did?" we said.

Ace didn't answer. Frustrated and defeated, we left him— Ace Cohen, blowing the outlines of asteroids apart.

.   .   .

They were all heroes to us, every single one of Russia's oppressed. We'd seen *Gulag* on cable television, and learned that for escapes across vast snowy tundras, two prisoners would invite a third to join, so that they could eat him along the way. We were moved by this as boys, and fantasized about sacrifice, wondering which of our classmates we'd devour.

Our parents were active in the fight for the refuseniks' freedom in the 1980s, and every Russian Jew was a refusenik, whether he wanted to be or not. We children donated our reversible-vested three-piece suits to help clothe Jewish unfortunates of all nations. And when occasion demanded, we were taken from our classes and put on buses to march for the release of our Soviet brethren.

We got our own refusenik in Greenheath right after Zvi's assault. Boris was the janitor at a Royal Hills yeshiva. He was refilling the towel dispenser in the faculty lounge when he heard of our troubles. Boris was Russian and Jewish, and he'd served in Brezhnev's army and the Israeli one to boot. He made his sympathies known to the teachers from Greenheath, voicing his outrage over our plight. That very Friday, a space was made in the Chevy Nova in which they carpooled while listening to Mishna on tape.

Boris came to town for a Shabbos, and then another, and had he slept twenty-four hours a day and eaten while he slept, he still couldn't have managed to be hosted by a fraction of the families that wanted to house and feed him and then feed him more.

The parents were thrilled to have their own refusenik—a menial laborer yet, a young man who pushed a broom for a living. They hadn't been so excited since the mothers went on an AMIT tour of the Holy Land and saw Jews driving buses and a man wearing tzitzit delivering mail. Boris was Greenheath's own Sharansky, and our parents gave great weight to his dire take on our situation. His sometimes-fractured English added its own gravity to the proceedings. "When hooligan gets angry," he would say, "when drinking too much, the anti-Semite will charge."

The first, informal self-defense class was given the day Boris was at Larry Lipshitz's playing Intellivision hockey and teaching Larry to smoke. It ended with Larry on the basement floor, the wind knocked out of him and a sort of wheeze coming from his throat. "How much?" he said to Boris. "How much what?" was Boris's answer. He displayed a rare tentativeness, which Larry might have noticed if he hadn't been trying to breathe. "For the lesson," Larry said. And here was the wonder of America, the land of opportunity. In Russia, if you punched someone in the stomach, you did it for free. A monthly rate was set, and Larry spread the word.

That was also the day that Barry Pearlman was descended upon by our nemesis as he left Vardit's Pizza and Falafel. His take-out order was taken. The vegetarian egg rolls (a staple of all places kosher, no matter the cuisine) were bitten into. A large pizza and a tahini platter were spread over the street. Barry was beaten, and then, as soon as he was able, he raced back into the store. Vardit, the owner, wiped the sauce from little Pearlman. She remade his order in full, charging only the pizza to his account. The Pearlmans didn't want trouble. The police were not called.

. . .

Barry Pearlman was the second to sign up. Then came the Kleins and cockeyed Shlomo, whose mother sent him because of the current climate, though really she wanted him to learn to defend himself from us.

Our rabbis at school needed to approve of the militant group we were forming. They remembered how Israel was founded with the aid of Nili and the Haganah and the undergrounds of yore. They didn't much approve of a Jewish state without a messiah, but they gave us permission to present our proposal to Rabbi Federbush, the founder of our community and the dean of our yeshiva.

His approval was granted, but only grudgingly. The old man is not to be blamed. Karate, he knew nothing of; the closest sport he was familiar with was wrestling, and this from rabbinic lore—a Greco-Roman version. His main point of protest, therefore, was that we'd be wrestling the uncircumcised publicly and in the nude. When the proposal was rephrased and he was told that we were being trained to battle the descendants of Amalek, who attacked the Israelites in the desert; that we were gearing up to face the modern-day spawn of Haman (cursed be his name); when told it was to fight the Anti-Semite, he nodded his head, understanding. "Cossacks," he said, and agreed.

. . .

It wasn't exactly a pure martial art, but an amalgam of Israeli Krav Maga, Russian hand-to-hand combat, and Boris's own messy form of endless attack. He showed us how to fold a piece of paper so it could be used to take out an eye or open a throat, and he told us always to travel with a circuit tester clipped to our breast pocket like a pen. When possible, Boris advised us, have a new gun waiting at each destination. He claimed to have learned this during a stint in the Finger of God, searching out Nazis in Argentina and then—acting as a military tribunal of one—finding them guilty and putting a bullet between their eyes.

We were taught to punch and kick, to stomp and bite, while the mainstay of all suburban martial-arts classes—when you can avoid confrontation, you do it—was removed. Boris told us to hold our ground. "Worst cases," he said, "raise hand like in defeat and kick for ball."

After a few weeks of lessons, we began to understand the power we had. Boris had paired Larry Lipshitz, that wisp of a boy, with Aaron, the middle Blum. They went at it in Larry's backyard, circling and jabbing with a paltry amount of rage. Boris stood off to the side, his arms resting on his paunch—a belly that on him was the picture of good health, as if it were the place from which all his strength emanated, a single muscle providing power to all the other parts.

Boris spat in the grass and stepped forward. "You are fighting," he said. "Fight." He put his foot to Aaron's behind and catapulted him into his opponent. "Friends later. Now win." Larry Lipshitz let out a yawp befitting a larger man and then, with speed and with grace, he landed the first solid roundhouse kick we'd seen delivered. It was no sparring partner's hit, but a shoulder fake and all-his-might strike, the ball of Lipshitz's bare foot connecting with Aaron's kidney. Larry didn't offer a hand. He stepped back like a champion and raised his fists high. Aaron hobbled to the nearest tree and displayed for us the first fruits of our training. He dropped his pants, took aim, and, I tell you, it was nothing less than water to wine for us when Aaron Blum peed blood.

.   .   .

It's curious that the story most often used to inspire Jewish battle readiness is that of Masada, an episode involving the last holdouts of an ascetic Israelite sect, who committed suicide in a mountain fortress. The battle was fought valiantly, though without the enemy present. Jews bravely doing harm to themselves. The only Roman casualties died of frustration in their encampment below—eight months in the desert spent building a ramp to storm fortress walls for a slaughter, and the deed already done when they arrived.

When Israeli army recruits complete basic training, they climb up that mountain and scream out into the echo, "A second time Masada won't fall." Boris made us do the same over the edge of Greenheath Pond, a body of water whose circulation had slowed, a thick green soup that sent back no sound.

.   .   .

Mostly, the harassment was aimed at the Blum boys and their house. I don't know if this was because of their proximity to the Anti-Semite's house, the call to the police, or the Anti-Semite's public slap in the face. I sometimes can't help thinking that the Blum boys were chosen as targets because they looked to the bully as they looked to me: enticingly victimlike and small. Over time, an M-80 was used to blow up the Blum mailbox, and four tires were slashed on a sensible Blum car. A shaving-cream swastika was painted on their walkway, but it washed away in the rain before anyone could document its existence.

When we ran into the Anti-Semite, insults were inevitably hurled, and punches thrown. Larry took a thrashing without managing his now-legendary kick. Shaken, he demanded his money's worth of Boris, and made very clear that he now feared for his life. Boris shrugged it off. "Not so easy," he assured him. "Shot and lived. Stabbed and lived. Not so easy to get dead."

My father witnessed the abuse. He came upon the three Blum boys crawling around and picking up pennies for the right to cross the street—the bully and his friends enforcing. My father scattered the boys, all but the three Blums, who stood there red in the face, hot pennies in their hands.

The most severe attack was the shotgun blast that shattered the Blums' bay window. We marked it as the start of dark days, though the shells were packed only with rock salt.

. . .

We stepped up our training and also our level of subterfuge. We memorized kata and combinations. We learned to march in lockstep, to run, leap, and roll in silence.

Lying on our backs in a row with feet raised, heads raised, and abdomens flexed, we listened to Boris lecture while he ran over us, stepping from stomach to stomach, as if crossing a river on stones. Peace, Boris insisted, was maintained through fear. "Do you know which countries have no anti-Semite?" he asked. We didn't have an answer. "The country with no Jew."

The struggle would not end on its own. The bully would not mature, see the error of his ways, or learn to love the other. He would hate until he was dead. He would fight until he was dead. And unless we killed him, or beat him until he thought we had killed him, we'd have no truce, no peace, no quiet. In case we didn't understand the limitations of even the best-case scenario, Boris explained it to us again. "The man hits. In future he will hit wife, hit son, hit dog. We want only that he won't hit Jew. Let him go hit someone else."

Despite all the bumps pushed back into foreheads and the braces freed from upper lips, I'm convinced our parents thought our training was worth the effort. Our mothers brought frozen steaks to press against black eyes and stood close as our fathers tilted our chins and hid smiles. "Quite a shiner," they would say, and they could hardly stand to give up staring when the steaks covered our wounds.

Along with the training injuries, we had other setbacks. One was a tactical error when, post–shotgun blast, we went as a group to egg the Anti-Semite's house. Shlomo thought he heard a noise and yelled, "Anti-Semite!" in warning. We screamed back, dropped our eggs, and fled in response. This all took place more than a block away from the house. We hadn't even gotten our target in sight.

We weren't cohesive. We knew how to move as a group but not as a gang.

We needed practice.

After two thousand years of being chased, we didn't have any hunt in us.

.   .   .

We sought help from Chung-Shik through Yitzy—an Israeli with an unfortunate heritage. Yitzy's parents had brought him to America with the last name Penis, which even among kind children doesn't play well. We teased Yitzy Penis ruthlessly, and as a result he formed a real friendship with his Gentile neighbor Chung-Shik, the only Asian boy in town. Both showed up happily, Yitzy delighted at being asked to bring his pal along.

And so we proposed it, our plan.

"Can we practice on you?" we asked.

"Practice what?" Chung-Shik said amiably, Yitzy practically aglow at his side.

When no one else answered, Harry spoke. "A reverse pogrom," he said.

"A what?"

"We just want to menace you," Harry said. "Chase you around a bit as a group. You know, because you're different. To get a feel for it."

Chung-Shik looked to his friend. You could see we were losing him, and Yitzy had already lost his smile.

That's when Zvi pleaded, almost a cry of desperation: "Come on, you're the only different kid we know."

Yitzy held Chung-Shik's stare, the Asian boy looking back, not scared as much as disappointed.

"Chase me instead," Yitzy said, sort of pantomiming that he could be Chung-Shik and Chung-Shik could be him, switch off the yarmulke and all.

We abandoned the idea right then. It wouldn't be the same.

. . .

Our failed offensive got back to Boris, as well as the reverse pogrom that wasn't, the continuing rise in Blum-related trouble, and chases home from school. The rock salt still stung us all.

We met in the rec room of the shul. Boris had swiped a filmstrip and accompanying audiocassette from the yeshiva he worked at in Royal Hills. He advanced the strip in the projector, a single frame every time the tape went *beep*. We knew the film well. We knew when the image would shift from the pile of shoes to the pile of hair, from the pile of bodies to the pile of teeth to the pile of combs. The film was a sacred teaching tool brought out only on Yom Hashoah, the Holocaust memorial day.

Each year, the most memorable part was the taped dramatization, the soundman's wooden blocks clop-clopping, the sound of those boots coming up the stairs. First they dragged off symbolic father and mother. And then, *clop, clop, clop,* those boots marched away.

The lights still dimmed, we would form two lines—one boys, one girls. We marched back to class this way, singing *"Ani Ma'amin"* and holding in our heads the picture they'd painted for us: six million Jews marching into the gas chambers, two by two; a double line three million strong and singing in one voice, "I believe in the coming of the Messiah."

Boris did not split us into two quiet lines. He did not start us on a moving round of that song, or the equally rousing "We Are Leaving Mother Russia," with its coda, "When they come for us, we'll be gone." After the film, he turned the lights back on and said to us, yelled at us, "Like sheep to the slaughter. Six million Jews is twelve million fists." And then he segued from fists and Jewish fighting to the story of brave Trumpeldor, who, Boris claimed, lost an arm in the battle of Tel Hai and then continued fighting with the one.

Galvanized, we went straight to the Anti-Semite's house. Zvi Blum, beaten, bothered, dug a hunk of paving stone out of the walkway to avenge his family's bay window. He tossed that rock with all his might. Limited athlete that he was, it hooked left and hit the wall of the house with a great bang. We fled. Still imperfect, still in retreat, we ran with euphoria, hooting and hollering, victorious.

. . .

A newfound energy emerged at the start of the next class, which was also the start of a new session. We lined up to pay Boris what was now a quarterly fee. He took three months' worth of cash in one hand, patted us each on the back with the other, and said, "Not yet leaders, but you've turned into men." Boris even said this to the Conservative boy, though it was Elliot's first lesson. He then addressed us regarding our successful mission. "Anti-Semite will come back harder," he said, declaring that only a strong offense would see this conflict to its end. Pyrotechnics were in order.

We ventured out to the turnpike that marked the border of our town. In the alley behind ShopRite, we worked on demolitions following recipes from Boris's training and inspired by some pages torn from an Abbie Hoffman book. We made smoke bombs that didn't smoke, and firebombs that never burned. And though we suspected that the recipes themselves were faulty, Boris shook his head as if we'd never learn.

We stuck with our bomb making, working feverishly, with Boris timing each attempt and at intervals yelling, "Too late, already dead." Then Elliot stood up with a concoction of his own, a bottle with a rag stuffed in the top, and announced, "This is how you build a bomb."

To prove it, he lit the rag, arced back, and threw the bottle. We watched it soar, easily traceable by its fiery tail. We heard it hit and the sound of glass and then nothing. "So what," Aaron said. "That's not a bomb. By definition, it has to go *boom*!" We went back to work until Boris said, "Lesson over," and a yellow light began to chip at the darkness in the sky, a warm yellow light and smoke. "Not a bomb," Elliot said, looking proud and terrified in equal measure. His bottle, we discovered, had hit the Te-Amo Cigar & Smoke Shop. It had ignited the garbage in the rear of the store. The drive-through window was engulfed in flames. "Simplest sometimes best," Boris said. And then: "Class dismissed." We started to panic, and he said, "Fire could be from anything." Right then, his pocket full of our money, and already in full possession of our hearts and heads, Boris walked off. He walked toward the burning store, so close to the flames that we covered our eyes. True to his teachings, Boris didn't turn and run. He didn't stop, either. We know for sure that he went back to Royal Hills and worked another day. All our parents ever said was "green card," and we heard that Boris continued west to Chicago and built a new life.

.   .   .

Mr. Blum was still at the office. The three boys Blum were each manning a window at home and staring out into the dark. They had, on their own and in broad daylight, gone down that hill with toilet paper and shaving cream. They'd draped the trees and marked the sidewalks, unleashing on their target the suburban version of tar and feathers. Then they'd run up to their house and taken their posts, holding them through night-fall. When their mother pulled the car into the garage after her own long day at work, she saw only what the boys hadn't done. She made her way back down the driveway to the curb, where the garbage pails stood empty, one of them tipped by the wind. Basic responsibilities stand even in times of trouble. She had not borne three sons so that she'd have to drag garbage pails inside.

No one knew the quality of the Anti-Semite's night vision. The only claim that could be made in his defense is that until the lapse, the Blum boys had been the sole draggers of the garbage pails on every other trash day in memory. In the Blum boys' defense—and they would forever feel they needed one—three watched windows left one side of the house unguarded. All that said, the sound of metal pails being dragged up a gravel driveway brought the Anti-Semite racing out of the dark—and masked his approach for Mrs. Blum.

Mrs. Blum, of course, had not been in our class. She had no notion of self-defense and was wholly unfamiliar with weaponry. When this brute materialized before her, his arm already in motion, she did not assume a defensive posture. She did not raise her fists or prepare to lunge. What she did was turn at the last instant to get a look at the tiny leather wand sticking out from his swinging hand. She had never seen a blackjack before. When the single blow met with the muscles of her back, it sent a shock through her system so great that she saw a thousand pinpricks in her eyes and felt her legs give way completely. Connecticut or no, Mrs. Blum was a Jew. *"Shanda!"* she said to the boy, who was already loping off.

Oh, those poor Blums. As we had found Zvi, Zvi discovered his own mother—not hanging from a bolt, but curled in the grass. Inside the house, an ice pack in place and refusing both hospital and house call, Mrs. Blum told her sons what she'd seen.

"Shanda!" she said again. *"Busha!"*

The boys agreed. A shame and an embarrassment.

When their mother lifted the receiver to call the police, Aaron pressed his finger down into the cradle of the phone. Mrs. Blum looked at her son and then replaced the receiver as Aaron slid his finger away. "Not this time," he said. And this time, she didn't.

. . .

When my mother told my father what had happened, he didn't want to believe it. "Nobody ever wants to believe what happens to the Jews," she said, "not even us." My father simply shook his head. "Since when," my mother said, "do anti-Semites have limits? They will cross all lines. Greenheath no better." Then she, too, took to shaking her head. I was sorry I'd told her, sorry to witness her telling him. We'd known our parents would respond with hands to mouth and *oy vey iz mir*s, but none of us expected to see such obvious disillusionment with the world they'd built. I turned away.

Though we'd been abandoned, Boris's wisdom still held sway. We were going to see to it that the Anti-Semite never hit back again. "Anti-Semite school," Harry Blum called it, mustering a Boris-like tone. A boy who attacks a woman half his size, who had already attacked her son, would, if able, do the same thing again. We decided we would use Zvi as our siren—set him out in the middle of the lot at the public school, so that the Anti-Semite might be drawn by the irresistible call of the vulnerable Jew. The rest of us would stay hidden in those bushes and then fall on our enemy as one. But looking from face to face, taking in skinny Lipshitz and fat Beryl, the three Blums full of anger and without any reach, we realized that we couldn't defeat the Anti-Semite, even as a group.

Boris was right. It was true what he'd said about us. We were ready, we were raring, and we were useless without a leader. We went off like that, leaderless, to Ace Cohen's house.

. . .

Tears, mind you. We saw tears in Ace Cohen's eyes. He stopped playing his Asteroids and did not get back into bed. Little Mrs. Blum attacked—it was too much to bear. Such aggression, he agreed, needed to be avenged. "So you'll join us," we said, assuming the matter had been decided. But he wouldn't. He still didn't want any part of us. A singular matter, the blow to Mrs. Blum. And likewise a singular matter, he felt, was the act of revenge.

One punch is what he offered. "You've got me, my Heebie-Jeebies. But only for one swing." We pressed him for more. We begged leadership of him. He showed us his empty hands. "One punch," he said. "Take it or leave it."

. . .

Certain things went according to plan. When the Anti-Semite arrived, he showed up alone. That he passed on a Saturday, and in a mood to confront Zvi, we took as a sign of the righteousness of our scheme.

We'd already been hiding in those bushes all morning, skipping shul. Sore and stiff, we were sure that the creaking of our joints would give us away, that the sound of our breathing, as all our hearts raced, would reveal the trap we'd laid.

And Zvi—what can be said about that brave Blum, out there alone on the asphalt between the jungle gym and the bushes, cooking under the hot sun? Zvi was poised in his three-piece suit, a red yarmulke like a bull's-eye on top of his head.

The Anti-Semite immediately began to badger Zvi. Zvi, empowered, enraged, and under the impression that we would immediately charge, spewed his own epithets back. The moment was glorious. Little Zvi in his suit, addressing— apparently—the brass belt-buckle on that mountain of a bully, raised an accusing finger. "You shouldn't have," Zvi said. His words came out tough; they came out beautiful—so boldly that they reached us in the bushes, and clearly moved the Anti-Semite to the point of imminent violence.

The situation would have been perfect if not for one unfortunate complication: the small matter of Ace Cohen's resistance. Ace Cohen was unwilling to budge. We begged him to charge with us, to rescue Zvi. "Second thoughts," he said. "A fine line between retaliation and aggression. Sorry. I'll need to see some torment for myself." We implored him, but we didn't charge alone. We all stayed put until push came to shove, until the Anti-Semite started beating Zvi Blum in earnest, until Zvi—his clip-on tie separated from his neck—hit the ground with a thud.

Then we sprang out of the bushes, on Ace's heels. We had the Anti-Semite surrounded, and Zvi pulled free with relative ease.

Ace Cohen, three inches taller and fifty pounds heavier, faced the bully down.

"Keep away" is all Ace said. Then, without form or chi power, his feet in no particular stance, Ace swung his fist so wide and so slowly that we couldn't believe anyone might fail to get out of the way. But maybe the punch just looked slow, because the bully took it. He caught it right on the chin. He took it without rocking back—an exceptional feat even before we knew that his jaw was broken. He remained stock-still for a second or two. Not a bit of him moved except for that bottom jaw, which had unhinged like a snake's and made a solid quarter turn to the side. Then he dropped.

Ace pushed his way through the circle we'd formed. It closed right back up around the Anti-Semite, bloodied and now writhing before us.

As I watched him, I knew I'd always feel that to be broken was better than to break—my failing. I also knew that the deep rumble rolling through us was only nerves, a sensitivity to imagined repercussion, as if a sound were built into revenge.

What we really shared in that instant was simple. Anyone who stood with us that day will tell you the same. With the Anti-Semite at our feet, confusion came over us all. We stood there looking at that crushed boy. And none of us knew when to run.

Peep Show

Allen Fein is on his way to Port Authority when he stubs his toe and scuffs his shoe—puts a nick in a five-hundred-dollar investment. He pulls out a handkerchief and spit-shines his toe cap, cursing with every pass of the cloth.

The scuffing, the nick, has bumped Allen from the flow to which he is accustomed. And he looks around Forty-second Street at the gentrified theaters and the wholesome shops, the kind a family can enter in the bright light of day. Where are all the hucksters who used to stand outside promising Nirvana and shaken booty, forbidden acts and creamy thighs? So busy has Allen been with his own transformation that he's missed the one going on around him.

He blushes at the thought, wondering how little Ari Feinberg had ever become Allen Fein, Esq., in fancy oxblood wing tips. When had he become a grown man, on his way home to a loving wife, a pregnant wife, a beautiful blond Gentile wife, who laughed when he didn't know how to work the Christmas lights, who bought a candle with a picture of Jesus on it when it came time for the memorial for his father? ("They were out of the little white ones," Claire had said. "Can't you just turn Jesus toward the wall?")

Allen straightens his tie and picks up his briefcase. He takes another look around and asks himself, As polished, as straight, as on the up-and-up as Forty-second Street now appears, is it still the same inside?

And then the man says it.

"Buddy," he says. "Mac," he says. "Upstairs. Girls. Live girls inside."

"What?" Allen says, catching the sign in the window: a giant neon token with "25¢" flashing in its center.

"That's right, buddy," the man says. "Twenty-five cents for a spherical miracle. New York's only three-hundred-and-sixty-degree all-around stage. Just follow the stairs, you can't get lost—all the arrows lead to one place."

And Allen goes in, glancing only for a second to see if fate has mustered an office mate or neighbor to descry his ascent. He heads into a stairwell and makes his way to the second floor.

When he enters the hall, he faces a towering figure behind a counter. Behind this giant, the hallway opens into a large room containing a single massive pillarlike structure, with doors to individual booths spaced evenly all around.

Allen smiles at the man as if the two are in on a joke, as if his visit is an understandable bit of mischief, the kind of thing he could tell Claire about. Yes, if he feels guilty enough, he'll tell Claire he went inside. Allen fishes out a quarter and places it on top of the counter.

"A dollar," the man says.

"It says a quarter."

"It's a dollar," the man says. He does not return Allen's smile.

Fumbling with his wallet, Allen pulls out a five-dollar bill and takes five tokens—too bashful to ask for change.

.   .   .

"Touch," she says. She is looking right at him; she can see him. This is not how Allen Fein remembers past visits, not with the women staring back. There are four women seated on a carpeted platform, and all, eyeing him, make the same offer. "Touch," they say. "Touch." Well, three of the women say it. The fourth—sitting in a cheap plastic lawn chair, too wide for it, her thighs, cut in half, drooping, like her breasts, in languid arcs toward the floor—is reading a book. She's got glasses on and is holding a page, ready to turn it, and Allen knows the motion will be slow and lazy, as weary as her posture.

They are all naked, or almost so. The second woman wears a bra, the third panties, and the fourth has the book and glasses. It is the first one who is, to Allen, beautiful.

He has not set foot in a peep show since boyhood, but he recalls almost everything from then. He remembers shivering so badly that his teeth chattered, his hands pressed between his legs for warmth. He'd been afraid that he might freeze to death, actually expire from excitement. And he'd often indulged this nightmare, squandered precious viewing time on the darker fantasy of dropping dead right there in the booth. Allen remembers the old setup. The sound of a token dropping and then the labored spin of gears. He remembers the strip of light at the bottom of the window frame as the wooden partition was drawn up into the wall. Behind thick glass—smudged and fingerprinted, always fogged with heavy breath—were the women. They danced as if they cared, moving to titillate the observer.

The individual booths are more or less the same. It's the windows that are different. Allen is shocked to find that the glass is gone. The women just sit on their chairs, vivid, looking back.

The stage is circular and completely surrounded by the inner wall of the booths. Many of the partitions are raised, and

Allen can see men in their compartments at all angles. One middle-aged, broad-headed voyeur is clearly masturbating with vigor. Allen catches the eye of a Latino man off to the side, wearing the very same tie he is. Allen puts a hand on his chest and feels the tie pulsing along with his heart. The Latino man, such a good-looking man, turns away from Allen and makes eye contact with the woman in the bra.

She stands up and walks over to the man, and his hands come out through the window, penetrating the fantasy world. Allen has never seen it broached before—the world of dreams cracked open.

.   .   .

When the first girl looks at Allen, he feels unworthy to watch. He can hardly bear having her acknowledge him. He wants to ask her what she is staring at. "Can I help you?" he would have said if they had been anywhere else. The girl is perfection, and Allen wants her desperately. It's a feeling so pure that he wants to cry. How terribly unfair that his whole self aches because of the shape of a shoulder, the soft line of a hip. Allen stares at the girl's legs, a deep black against the whiteness of the chair, and then up at the trained beckoning in her face. There is the glow of real personality behind the staged.

"Touch," she says. And Allen wants to touch her—to see if she is real. But he hasn't yet responded, and the girl is moving toward him, long and graceful, the woman of his dreams.

Allen is shaking again, as he did when he was a boy. And why shouldn't he be? A loyal husband, who, reaching out, touching, had always honored his vows.

He does not move his hands or his fingers, just holds them against her wonderful skin, so warm, almost hot. The girl takes

Allen's hands in her own, presses them to her chest, and massages. It calms him. She does this like an expert, a masseuse, someone trained in an art. Allen hasn't been so aroused in years. He wants to climb through the small window to be with this woman. But the partition starts to come down. His time has run out. In the split second he has to make his choice, Allen takes back his hands.

Leaning up against the wall in a panic, Allen tells himself that the fondling of this woman was an aberration, just like his coming up those stairs.

He had only wanted a peep. He'd gone up the stairs a loyal husband and lover, a working man on his way home to the burbs. And now, minutes later, a different man emerges: a violator of girls and wives and matrimonial bonds. Allen considers leaving the booth, though his legs feel hollow and unsteady. And there is also his erection, diabolically hard, bringing to mind all the basest descriptions in pornographic magazines.

Allen is so close to climax that he is afraid to move. He wants to get away without having to face the enormity of his pleasure. He remains still, his hand clutched tightly around the tokens, and thinks of Claire waiting at the bus stop, the seat belt stretched over the arc of her stomach, a chamomile tea steaming in her travel mug. But then there is the girl on the other side. So wonderful. Her legs and skin. The way, the skill, with which she touched. The idea of her is so enticing, it pushes him past control. Allen lets go and lets the shame rush in and fill the emptiness, so that even his hollow legs feel solid and full.

Immediately, there is plotting. Already the deceit grows. What to do with his boxer briefs? And to ride the bus to Parsippany this way, to face Claire, soiled. She could drop him at the gym. The gym before dinner, that is the plan. But his erection endures. Allen is neither so old that it should disappear in an

instant nor so young that it should remain, and in such a pro-
nounced and steadfast state.

Then again, he thinks, why should it fade when that angel
of a girl is so near and there are four more tokens? He has already
crossed the threshold and made his way inside. The erection
builds strength and, Allen fears, may never go away. He cannot
walk out in this state. And he admits to himself that if he didn't
ever have to leave, if it meant irretrievably losing the outside
world, he would sacrifice it all if only that siren would stand up
from her chair, take his hands, and guide them over her body
once more. But he won't allow himself such an indulgence. He
will put in the token, but he will not touch. He will look at his
shoes and the scuff mark that damned him. This is how he will
occupy himself, without a whit more enjoyment. He will use up
what he paid for, but the penance begins right now.

. . .

Allen drops the second token in the slot and, closing his
eyes and hearing the partition rise, falls against the wall of the
booth.

There is silence. He waits, counting in his head. A dollar
doesn't buy much, and soon the window will close.

"Hey!"

He hears it, the voice deep, raspy, and, he thinks, rather
accusatory. "Hey, you. Feinberg. You want to touch?" Allen
knows who it is. But it takes some time, an understandable
pause. "Touch, Feinberg? You want to cop a feel?"

He raises his eyes and goes cold. There, in the first chair,
looking the same, though fifteen years older, is Rabbi Mann.
He is naked and fat, his chest hairy. Mann has become so over-
weight that his masculine breasts are bigger than the girl's.

Down the row are three other rabbis from his old school.

Rabbi Rifkin sits in the second chair, wearing boxers, a bleached-out blue. Then there's Rabbi Wolf, wearing tzitzit, the once white fringes now yellow against the chair. In the last seat is Rabbi Zeitler, a tractate spread across his lap, his glasses black and thick-lensed, so that his eyes seem tiny and his head deeply notched. Zeitler adjusts his glasses, pushing them higher on his nose.

Amazed at himself for not passing out or losing, immediately, his mind, Allen wishes that his shrink, Dr. Springmire, were there to help him along. The rabbis' return is a lot for him to process. He has worked hard at breaking from their world and he doesn't remember ever wanting it back.

Rabbi Mann stamps a foot against the floor. "Down to business, Feinberg. Should I come over so you can lay a hand on me? Do you want me to come over by you?"

Allen grabs the window frame, scratches at the groove in the top, trying to drag the partition down. "Please, Rabbi. Sit. Do sit."

"Of me you don't want a pinch?" Mann puts on a falsetto. He holds up his arms and waves his fingers. He is trying to look dainty. "I'm not so good as the pretty girl with the long legs? Too hairy? Too Jewish to be touched by the big-shot lawyer? By Mr. Ari-Allen-Feinberg-Fein?"

"That's not it," Allen says. "Not at all. I wasn't going to touch her again. I was already done."

"Not true, Feinberg. I know better. Ari Feinberg isn't satisfied. He never is." Rabbi Mann addresses the other rabbis. "But does he ever stay to finish? No, he always turns to run."

A good idea, Allen thinks. He spins and makes a rush for the door.

"Hold it, Feinberg. Turn around. Look at me. Listen for a second."

Allen drops his hands, turns, looks, listens.

"Always so emotional," Rabbi Mann says, leaning forward so that his testicles hang off the end of the chair. "Always acting without thinking and chasing around after your own heart." Rabbi Rifkin nods in agreement. Rifkin has always agreed. "Listen, Fein—I'll even call you by your new name. Turn on your lawyer's head, Fein, and try to follow some logic. Do you think if I'm here, if I've brought the other rabbis and we're sitting up here like at the *shvitz* bath, that you can so easily tiptoe out the door? Use a bit of *sachel*"—Rabbi Mann taps at his head—"and deal!"

Always more. The rabbis have always wanted more from Fein than Fein gives. But is he not dealing spectacularly well? Is he screaming "This can't be happening!"? No. He is listening with a fair amount of respect. After all, it's an invasion of privacy and a Halachic crime. Whatever the rabbis think, the tokens, the neon signs, the man in the street all promise live girls—which the rabbis are not. They are, in effect, stealing from him with every second they sit onstage.

The rabbis don't seem to mind. They sit and stare, and Allen stares back. He is waiting for his token to run out and the partition to lower.

When it doesn't, Allen asks them a question. He tries to sound unflustered, but his voice is all schoolboy angst, the question a plea.

"Why," Allen says, "doesn't the partition come down?"

Mann is as aggravated as he was when trying to teach the boy Talmud fifteen years before. "That's the kind of idiocy I'm talking about. Do you think, Fein—do you really think that the window is supposed to close?"

"No," Allen says, his tone pitiful. "I don't think it's ever going to close."

"So frustrating!" Mann is shouting now. "You know it won't stay open forever as well as you know it won't close too soon. You've got a good head, Fein. So tell me why you're always acting like a dummy."

"You wonder why I don't talk to you? Listen to yourself, Rabbi. Always on the attack."

"What, I should hold you up as an example? Say that Fein made the right choice when he decided it was easier to live without God? Congratulate you on changing your name so that the *goyishe* restaurant man doesn't make you repeat your reservations? Fein, who goes to live in a town where there are no troubles and no Jews, so his son will be able to play soccer carefree on Shabbos morning?"

"It's a boy?" Allen interrupts. "Claire's having a boy?"

"I don't know! Look at you, always worrying over the tiny details. What about the fact that it won't be a Jew?"

"I'm all right with that," Allen says.

This is when another partition, directly behind the row of rabbis, opens. Allen is not surprised to see Dr. Springmire, his psychologist, standing there, scratching at his short secular beard. A witness. Mann has called a witness.

"First a token," the doctor says to his patient.

"A token?" Allen says.

"I think it would be best if you paid for my peep. Thus far in your therapy, we've constructed a relationship based partly on financial remuneration. We dare not put that trust in jeopardy, especially in a situation as peculiar as this." He offers an apologetic smile.

Mann rolls his eyes as Allen inserts a token on Springmire's behalf.

"Is Fein all right with his transformation, Mr. Doctor?"

"He will be," Springmire says. "He has come a long way, and one day he will, I'm convinced, adjust to the life he has made—it is a very nice life. He is a very nice man."

"Did I say he wasn't?" Rabbi Mann strains, twists in his

chair to face the doctor behind him. "I'm here for that very reason. I want to know what makes a nice boy forget God. What makes a boy with a nice job and a nice life never question how he came to such comfort? What makes such a darling boy—with such a darling wife waiting for him at home—climb the stairs into a place like this to fondle a young girl who must sell her body to live?"

It is Allen who answers. "It's you." He points a finger and reaches through the window.

Rabbi Zeitler looks up from his book and says, absent-mindedly, "Touch?"

"It's you who made me this way," Allen says. "I came here because of you." And with a fresh sense of injustice, he recalls Mann's classroom, and how the rabbi would bring a heavy fist down against his desk, condemning student after student for matters that surely could be settled only in the world to come.

"Really?" Mann says, a big smile on his face. "And all the time I thought it was the other way around."

"What choice was I left with, Rabbi? When I used to play at Benji Wernik's house, the grandson to the Galitzia Rebbe, he used to pull filthy magazines from the space between his father's bookcase. This is where his father hid them. What am I to do if I learned the facts of life from Simcha Wernik's magazines?"

Dr. Springmire is raising a finger. "If I may interject, it is normal to masturbate. Healthy, even. Such pictures are of no importance if in the possession of an adult man."

"But the son of the Galitzia Rebbe. A wise man. A teacher of high school science. What is a boy raised in a world of absolutes to do when he is faced with contradictions?" Allen turns his attention back to Mann. "You painted for us the most beautiful picture of Heaven, Rabbi, then left us to discover we'd all end up in Hell. Some room—maybe if you'd left us some room."

Rabbi Mann is fed up. He waves a fist, the loose flesh of his upper arm shaking obscenely. "You should have questioned, Fein. That is what intelligent people do. They don't throw their religion away. They don't turn into the sick people who first shook their faith."

"I'm not sick!" Allen yells. "And I didn't throw anything away! You want truth and justice and for everything to fit in its place. But some things are in between, Rabbi. They are not right or wrong. Only natural."

"Who's saying different? There are many ugly vices in the world." Mann rubs his palms along his thighs. "Did I need to come here for you to admit this to yourself? To learn that you abandoned God because the world is not the way you wanted it to be?"

"That's not what I said."

Rabbi Mann exhales. "Then what did you say?"

"That I left religion because of people like you."

"Me," Mann says, voice booming. "Me?" Then, controlling himself: "If that's what you want to tell yourself, then that's what I wanted to know."

The partition moves down easily, as if oiled. Allen, with two tokens left, grabs at the door and is sliding the bolt open when he understands one thing. The partition will rise up twice more. Where the rabbis are involved, there is always a path to be followed. Either you stay on it or you stray into darkness: This is the choice that they offer. And, much as Allen feels bitter and lied to for all these years, he half wishes he could live in their realm, where a man is religious or he is not, a good husband or bad. A place where the scales of justice always dip to one side and where the rabbis know what to do with Simcha Wernik, a clean man with a dirty magazine.

Running his thumb along the face of a token, Allen bolts the door again. He will face his teachers; he will not run or hide, only to find himself haunted. He does not want to suffer the rabbis when he pulls the car into the garage or discover them in the basement every time a fuse blows. Allen checks his watch. There is time enough to spend his tokens and reach the bus. And maybe it will be the girls again. Maybe Mann is gone. He said he found what he wanted to know.

.   .   .

Steeling himself, Allen drops in a token. As the partition goes up and he sees the round leg of a woman, an older woman, he is overjoyed—as simple as that. It's over. When Allen realizes that this woman is his mother, he knows that he is wrong. Claire sits next to her, in a pair of panties, only the sides visible because of her gigantic pregnant belly. Many of the partitions are open, and Allen can see the men, their arms moving, their expressions wide-eyed, as if hypnotized. One man is wearing a yarmulke. It's Benji Wernik, grandson of the Galitzia Rebbe.

Allen's mother is wearing stockings and garters. In the place where other such women keep tips, she has a wad of Kleenex.

"Do you need some tissue, Ari? Did you remember to bring?" She gets up to hand him some.

"Sit," he says. "Mother, sit down!"

"What, and let you spoil a fancy hanky? Let alone an expensive suit."

"Mother, please, what are you saying?"

"I'm saying that I washed your underwear every day and know from such things." Allen's mother, who hates the very idea of his Gentile wife, who declared her invisible on the day of the wedding, actually leans toward Claire and touches her hand. "He wants to know of what I speak," his mother says.

"Underwear stiffer than starched, I scrubbed. Underwear that would shatter if you dropped them to the floor. I tell you, if the Russians had dropped a nuclear bomb when I was in that basement, I would have been safe surrounded by his dirty *gatkes*."

"You knew?"

"Of course. I'm a mother. What, you are the first in the world to do such a thing?"

"It's normal. The doctor says so. The rabbi didn't even dispute it—and he knows it's a sin." Fein is backpedaling, explaining it all away.

"Who said it wasn't normal?" His mother speaks to his wife.

Claire shrugs and spreads her legs, giving Benji Wernik a better view.

"All I'm saying," his mother says, tucking the tissues back into place, "is to have some sense about it. Why ruin a good suit? Why ruin a good marriage . . ." And then she pauses.

Claire turns, waits. Allen waits even as he prays for the partition to drop. They all wait for his mother to finish the sentence: "Why ruin a good marriage, even if it's to her?" But she doesn't. Claire smiles and moves her hand, placing it on top of her mother-in-law's. She squeezes it and says, "So true."

Allen stands openmouthed. It's a concession from his wife, an act of betrayal by his mother. She has never before acknowledged anything that was not as she pleased.

"Is this what the rabbi means?" he asks them. "Is this how people learn to deal?"

But there is no time for an answer. The fourth dollar is spent and the window comes down.

. . .

Allen holds the last token lightly. How good it will feel to let it drop. He is actually eager to find the rabbi and Dr. Springmire waiting for him, eager to show them both that he is resigned to coping in a situation from which he gladly would have run. He wants to turn out his pockets, to hold up for them his empty hands. Allen presses the last token into the slot.

But the window opens onto an empty chair. The three others are filled with the women who were there when Allen arrived; only his beauty has gone. The second lady addresses him, her accent strong, a native of the Bronx.

"You're up," she says, and pats the empty seat.

Allen is already taking off his jacket and undoing his shoes. He uses one shoe to kick off the other, maybe for the first time since he was a boy in black Shabbos loafers, his father yelling at him not to break the backs.

When Allen is naked except for his watch, he reaches down and finds a handle on the wall in front of him. He takes hold of it, as if he has always known it was there, and opens his section of wall; the hinges, he assumes, are hidden on the other side.

Allen Fein steps up onto the stage and sits in the empty chair.

He is embarrassed, most especially because his erection persists. He covers it for a moment and then drops his hands.

When Allen hears the partition behind him open, he hopes that it's Claire. He does not want to be touched by his mother or by Rabbi Mann. He turns around gracefully and finds the Latino man wearing the familiar tie. This he can handle. In this way, he can bend.

"Touch?" Allen says.

The Latino man does not answer, but Allen understands

the man's wishes; he is surprised by his own sensitivity in knowing, an art of sorts.

Standing up, Allen walks toward the man. He moves slowly and with an air of detachment. Just the right amount, he feels, befitting an object of desire.

Everything I Know About
My Family on My Mother's Side

1. Watch the husband and wife walking down Broadway together. Even looking at their backs, even from a distance, you can see the wife is making big sweeping points, advising. There is wisdom being shared. But she is a kindly woman, the wife. You can see this, too. Because every few paces, the wife slows and reaches toward the husband, hangs an arm around his shoulder, and pulls him close. There is clearly love between them.

2. If we weave through the crowd with a little gusto, we'll make progress. If we take advantage of the pause when the two stand by a table of trinkets—bracelets and lighters and watches, all of them, oddly, embossed with the faces of revolutionaries—we get close enough to become suspicious of their relationship, about the nature of its husband-and-wifeness.

3. The two stop right in the middle of Canal Street. The wife faces the husband, and the point she argues is so large, it's as if the wife believes traffic will stop for it when the light changes, as if, should the cars roll on, it's worth being run down to see her point made.

It's then that we catch up, then that we're sure—as the woman smiles and hooks her arm through the man's, guiding him safely across—that the wife is not a wife and the husband not a husband.

4. What they are, it seems clear now, is boyfriend and girl-friend. And that girlfriend, upon closer inspection, seems to be a cat-eyed and freckle-faced Bosnian. Standing next to her, looking ten years older and with a mess of curly hair, the other one—the boyfriend one—is, we see, just a little Jew. And recognizing the face, taking it in, we see that the little Jew is me.

5. It's because of how they walk and talk, in the way their shoulders bump and how her lower back is held and released by him at every corner, that we assume a different type of inti-macy. There is an ease—a certain safety, you could call it—that just makes a person think husband and wife. From a distance, it just seemed another thing.

6. The argument that they—that is, that she and I—settle in the middle of Canal Street sounds, in a much truncated form, like this, with me earnest and at wit's end: "But what do you do if you're American and have no family history and all your most vivid childhood memories are only the plots of sitcoms, if even your dreams, when pieced together, are the snippets of movies that played in your ear while you slept?"

"Then," the girl says, "those are the stories you tell."

7.   Her family tree is written into the endpapers of a Bible whose leather cover has worn soft as a glove. She was raised in the house in which her mother was raised, and her mother's mother, and in which, believe it or not, her great-grandmother was born. Think of this: The ancient photos around her had grown old on the walls.

When the Bosnian came to America with her parents, they took the Bible, but the pictures, along with the still-living relatives in them, were left behind.

8.   We're still in the street, arguing over my family history gone lost, and I say what I always say to this girl who was swaddled in a quilt sewn from her grandmother's dresses: "Oh, look at me, my uncle shot Franz Ferdinand and started World War One, then Count Balthus came to Sarajevo to paint a portrait of my mother playing badminton in white kneesocks." For this, there's always a punch in the arm and a kiss to make up. This time, I also want a real answer.

9.   "What you do is tell the stories you have, as best you can."

"Even if they're about going to the mall? About eating bagel dogs and kosher pizza?"

"Yes," she says.

"You don't mean that."

"I don't mean that," she says. "You find better stories than that." And looking at me, frustrated, "You can't, not really, know nothing! Tell me about your mother. Tell me an anecdote right now."

"Everything I know about my family on my mother's side wouldn't even make a whole story." And she knows enough of me, my girl does, to know that it's true.

10. The Bosnian, my Bean—and, admittedly, that's what I call her—she fills me with confidence. I go from saying it's hopeless to telling her about the Japanese beetles, about the body in the stairwell, about the soldier with the glass eye. "You see," she says, "there is story after story. Plenty of history to tell."

11. My mother's father had two brothers, both of them long dead. My grandfather never told me about either brother. These are the stories he told me instead: "During Prohibition, we drank everything. Vanilla. Applejack. When I was down in Virginia, we used to go out to where the stills were hidden in the woods and buy moonshine. Always, you take a match to it first. If it burns white, you're all right. If it burns blue, then it's methanol. If it burns blue and you drink it, you go blind."

12. Applejack, it's just hard cider. My grandfather told me how to make it. You take fresh cider and you put it in a jar and throw in a bunch of raisins, for the sugar. You let it ferment, watching those raisins go fat over time. Then you put it in the freezer and you wait. Alcohol has a lower freezing point than water. When the ice forms, you take out the jar, you fish out the ice (or pour out the liquid), and what's not frozen, that's alcohol—easy as pie. I tried it one Thanksgiving, when suddenly, even in suburbia, cider abounds. I threw in the raisins. I waited and froze and skimmed and drank. I don't think I got drunk. I don't think anything happened. But neither did I go blind.

13. If you were to climb into my childhood head and look out from my childhood eyes, you'd see a world of Jews around

you: the parents, the children, the neighbors, the teachers—everyone a Jew, and everyone religious in exactly the same way. Now look across the street at the Catholic girl's house, and at the house next door to hers, where the Reform Jews live. Now what do you see? Is it a blur? An empty space? If you are seeing nothing, if your answer is nothing, then you are seeing as I saw.

14. Now that I'm completely secular, my little niece looks at me—at her uncle—through those old eyes. She asks my older brother sweetly, "Is Uncle Nathan Jewish?" Yes, is the answer. Uncle Nathan is Jewish. He's what we call an apostate. He means you no harm.

15. My great-grandfather gave up on religion completely. And my grandfather told me why he did. This is true, by the by. Not true in the way fiction is truer than truth. True in both realms.

16. What he told me is that his father and two other boys were up on the roof of a house in their village in Russia. One of the boys—not my great-grandfather—had to pee and peed off that roof. What he didn't see below him was a rabbi going by.

Like a story, every stream has an arc that has to come down somewhere. The boy pissed on the rabbi's hat. The three children were brought before the anointed party. They were, all three, soundly and brutally beaten. The punishment meted out was an injustice my great-grandfather couldn't abide. He thought, in Russian, in Yiddish, in his version, Fuck the whole lot, I'm done.

17. Up until this story, all I knew was that our family was from Gubernia. That's where we hailed from. And when I tell my sweet Bosnian, who also speaks some Russian, she shakes her head, looking sad, as if maybe everything I know really isn't enough. "*Gubernia* just means 'state,'" she says, "like a county. To say you were born in *gubernia* would be like saying you were born in *state*. As in, New York State or Washington State. To be from there is to be from everywhere."

"Or nowhere," I say.

18. It's when I'm asking my mother about the other side, about my grandmother's side, that she says, "Well, it's when Grandma's grandma, that is [and here, the middle-distance stare, the ticking off on fingers], when my mother's mother's mother came from Yugoslavia to Boston—" And that's when I stop her. Thirty-seven years old, and for the first time, in writing this, I find that my great-great-grandmother—my people—came from Yugoslavia. How does that not ever come up? I'm flabbergasted, and I want to call the Bosnian to say, "Hey, neighbor, it's me, Nathan. Guess what?" But she is not the person to call with such news—not anymore. That's how quickly things change. Some truths, you can hide forever, but when you finally face them, finally take a look . . . well, with me and the Bosnian, it's done.

19. About Yugoslavia, about the news, my mother doesn't pity me over stories suppressed. She says, "You have nothing to complain about. I had it worse in my not knowing." Her uncle, my grandfather's brother, died at age eight of a brain tumor. There was nothing to be done. A brain tumor killed the littlest brother of the three. My grandfather was twelve at the time, his middle brother ten, and his dead-of-a-brain-tumor brother eight. And my mother worried about every headache I had in my life. She worried about every little twitch and high fever in my childhood. She waited for the malady to start, the disease that eats the brains of young boys.

20. And then, in 2004—"That spring," my mother says—she drives up to Boston because Cousin Jack needs a new hip, a new shoulder, a new valve; she drives up to Boston because Cousin Jack is getting fitted for a replacement part. There she learns a different story from Jack, different from the one she's carried her whole life. My grandfather, all of twelve, was crossing Commonwealth Avenue with his littlest brother, with Abner, when a car came over the hill and clipped him. Knocked little Abner from my grandfather's grip. Abner got up. Abner looked fine, except for his right hand. A deep cut in the hand that might have been of concern to the driver had he taken a closer look. Instead, he got out of the car, stared at the little Jew boys looking fine enough, and drove off.

21. My grandfather led his brother home. Great-Grandma Lily (my grandfather's mother) screamed in shock. "A car? An accident? Look at this cut." She cleaned the wound. She wrapped the wound. And she made her littlest son lie down. She cleaned and wrapped, but she did not call a doctor. My great-grandfather did not call a doctor. It would get better. It would get better even after the fever took, even when, running up the arm, was a bright red line, an angry vein. The boy would mend, until he didn't, so that my grandfather's littlest brother died from nothing more than a cut to his hand. Lily would not recover. Her husband would not recover. My grandfather

would not recover. But, in a sense, they did. Because on the outside they did. Because it turned into a brain tumor. It turned into what was so clearly God's will and so clearly unstoppable, a malady that begs no other response than a *tfu-tfu-tfu*.

22. There were two brothers left. And then there was, a decade or so later, a world war. My grandfather, legally blind, could not be sent over. He was drafted, but worked an office job.

23. His office mate was a soldier with a glass eye. At night, this soldier would drink and drink, and then, when everyone was as drunk as he was, he'd pop out his regular glass eye and pop in one that, instead of an iris, contained one red swirl inside another—a bull's-eye. A little trick to get a laugh, to make the uninitiated think they'd had one too many, which they already had.

24. My grandfather's brother was killed in the war. His brother died fighting. That's how it was, until right now.

25. My favorite family story didn't come to me through blood. It's about Paul, my grandmother's father, and it came by way of Theo (who married Cousin Margot) and was, for the next thirty years, my grandfather's best friend. Inseparable. They were inseparable, those two.

26. "Your Great-Grandfather Paul, he had a bull's neck. Eighteen, nineteen inches around. He was a tough motherfucker."

Theo tells me this on the day we bury my grandfather. We're outside a restaurant near the graveyard; everyone else has already gone in. Theo and I stand in the parking lot. He stamps his feet against the cold. "One day, after work, me and your grandfather and Paul, we went to a bar for the train workers. We were sitting at the bar, the three of us, and the man right next to your great-grandfather, he turns to Paul and says, 'You know what the problem with this place is?' Your great-grandfather sizes him up. 'What's the problem?' he says. 'I'd like to know.' So the man tells him. 'Too many Jews,' he says. Your great-grandfather puts down his drink. He's still sitting, mind you. Still facing forward and seated on his barstool. Without even much of a look, he balls up a fist and he just pops the guy—crosswise— just clocks that guy right in the jaw. Sitting down! And then your great-grandfather picks up his drink like it's nothing, and he throws it back. One quick punch, and he knocked him out cold." Theo shakes his head in remembering. "That mutt just fell off his stool like a sack of corn."

27. And I can't even handle it, it's so good a story. "What'd you do?" I say. "What happened?" And Theo is laughing. "What do you think?" Theo says. "I said, 'Let's get the fuck out of here.' Then me and your grandfather, we grabbed Paul and got the hell out of that bar."

28. And what can I contribute to my own family history, what stories have I witnessed firsthand? I can tell you about breakfast. My grandfather cooked like nobody's business. And, above all, it was breakfast he did best. Burned coffee and burned eggs and bacon burned black. Bacon that we did not eat as a religious family—though our mouths watered at the smell. When

we stayed at my grandparents' (my parents, my brother, and me), we'd wake to a cloud of burned-bacon smoke filling the house. It would summon us, cartoonlike, lifting us from bed with a curling finger of smoke.

29. Right before the end of things, Bean and I walk to Greenpoint to buy chocolates at one of the Polish stores. We pass a Ukrainian grocery, which reminds Bean of her Ukie parts. She tells me of a great-uncle, a butcher, who slipped and fell into a vat of boiling hams. He was dead in an instant, leaving eight children behind. "Even your bad stories are good," I tell her. "A very bad story," she agrees. And I add, upon consideration, "That's possibly the least Jewish way to die." "Yes," she says. "Not the traditional recipe for Jews." And looking around at all the Polish stores, I agree. "Traditionally, yes, correct. Jews go in the oven. Pagans, burned at the stake. And Ukranian uncles . . ." "Boiled," she says. "Boiled alive."

30. Theo tells me this: When he was three, he was left alone in his family's little bungalow in Far Rockaway. "Still standing," he says. "They've torn down practically all of them, but that one still stands." In his parents' bedroom, under his father's pillow, he found a loaded gun. Theo took the gun. He aimed at the window, at the clock, and then took aim at the family dog, a sweet, dumb old beagle asleep next to the bed. He pulled the trigger; Theo shot that dog through his floppy ear. The bullet lodged in the floor. "You killed him?" I ask. "No, no, the dog was fine as fine can be—fine but for a perfect circle through that ear."

Sammy (the dog) just opened his sad, milky eyes, looked at Theo, and went back to sleep.

31. Cousin Jack stands with me while Theo tells that story. Jack doesn't believe it. "What about kickback?" he says. "You were all of three. Should have shot you across the room. You'd have a doorknob in your ass until this day."

"A .22," Theo says. "There doesn't have to be much kick. A .22 short wouldn't have to knock over a flea."

"Still," Jack says. "A little boy. Hard to believe it."

"I guess I handled it," Theo says, and looks off. And to me, there is nothing in that look but honesty. "I must have handled it," Theo says, "because I still remember the feel of that shot."

32. It is "the feel of that shot" that does it. It is "the feel of that shot" that undoes another sixty years for Jack. Because out of nowhere, he is talking again, Jack, who does not keep secrets—or keeps them for half a century, until suddenly the truth appears. "Terrible," Jack says. "It was a terrible phone call to get. I can still remember. I was the one who picked up the phone."

33. "What phone?" I say. "What call? What terrible?" I rush things out, desperate for any history to put things in place. I'm sure that I've already scared the story off with my eagerness, my panic. I'm sure it's about Abner, about the little boy dying.

"The call about your grandfather's brother."

"About Abner?" I say, because I can't keep my mouth shut, can't wait.

"No," he says. "About Bennie. The call from your grandfather to tell me Bennie had died."

34. Margot is now standing there, her arm hooked through Theo's, her face full of concern. "You got the call about Bennie being killed in the war?"

"Yes," Jack says. Then: "No."

"You didn't get it?" she says.

"I did. I got the call. But it wasn't the war."

"He was killed in the war," Margot says. "In Holland."

"He was buried in Holland," Jack says. "Not killed there. And he wasn't killed in the war. It was after."

"After."

"After the fighting. After the end of the war. His gun went off on guard duty."

"You always said," Margot says incredulously, "everyone always said: 'Killed in Holland during the war.'"

35. Jack puts a hand on my shoulder, hearing Margot but talking to me. "'Guard duty' is what your grandfather told me that day. 'An accident.' Then, a few months later, we're out in my garage—I remember this perfect. I'm holding a carburetor, and he takes it, and he's looking at it like it's a kidney or something, weighing it in his hand. 'It was a truck,' he says. 'Bennie asleep in the back, coming off guard duty. Something joggled, something fired, and Bennie shot through the head.'"

It's Theo who speaks: "That's one in a million, that kind of accident. Spent my life around guns."

"It is," Jack says. "One in a million. Maybe more."

36. What I'm thinking—and maybe it's the way my head works, maybe it's just the way my synapses fire—but in this Pat Tillman, quagmire-of-Iraq world, I'm thinking, I don't like the sound of it. And maybe I'm being truly paranoid. It is, as

I said, sixty years later. The idea that it already sounds funny, and already is the cut hand turned brain tumor, is not for me to think. And then Jack says, "I never did like the sound of it. That story never sat right."

37. Margot says, "I don't know why your grandfather never visited."

"There was talk," Jack says. "Right after. But then, like everything else in this family"—and no one has ever said such a thing before, no one ever acknowledged the not acknowledging—"it just got put away and then it was gone."

38. I am in Holland on book tour. I am at the Ambassade Hotel in Amsterdam, eating copious amounts of Dutch cheese and making the rounds. There is one day off. One day free if I want to see *The Night Watch* or the red lights or to go walk the canals and get high. My publisher, he offers me all these things. "No thank you," I say. "I'm going to Maastricht to visit a grave."

39. When you tell the Americans you are coming, the care-taker goes out and does something special. He rubs sand into the marker of your dead. The markers are white marble, and the names, engraved, do not show—white on white, a striking field of nameless stones. But with the sand rubbed, the names and the dates, they stand out. So you walk the field of crosses, looking for Jewish stars. When you find your star and see the toasted-sand warmness of the name, you feel, in the strangest way, as if you're being received as much as you're there to pay tribute. It's a very nice touch—a touch that will last until the first rain.

40. Do you want to know what I felt? Do you want to know if I cried? We don't share such things in my family—we don't tell this much even. Already I've gone too far. And put being a man on top of it; compound the standard secretiveness and shut-downness of my family with manhood. It makes for another kind of close-to-the-vest, another type of emotional distance, so that my Bosnian never knew what was really going on inside.

41. This happened at the bridge club, back in '84 or '85. My grandparents are playing against Cousin Theo and Joe Gor-back. (Margot never plays cards.) Right when it's old Joe's turn to be the dummy, he keels over and dies. The whole club waits for the paramedics and the gurney, and then the players play on—all but for my grandparents' table, short one man.

They wait on the director. Wait for instruction.

And Theo looks at my grandparents, and looks at his partner's cards laid out, and over at the dead man's tuna sand-wich, half-eaten. Theo reaches across for the untouched half. He picks it up and eats it. "Jesus, Theo" is what my grandfather says. And Theo says, "It's not like it's going to do Joe any good."

"Still, Theo. A dead man's sandwich."

"No one's forcing you," he says. "You're welcome to sit quiet, or you can help yourself to a fry."

42. My grandfather wasn't superstitious. But it's that half sand-wich, he's convinced, that brings it on Theo—a curse. That's what he says when Theo parks his car at the top of the hill over by the Pie Plate and forgets to put his emergency brake on. He's heading on down to the restaurant when he looks back up and sees his car lurch and start rolling. And he still claims it's the

fastest he ever ran in his life. Theo gets run over by his own Volvo. He breaks his back, though you'd never tell to look at him today.

43. My couch is ninety-two inches; it's a deep green three-cushion. It seats hundreds. But that's not why I got it. I got it because, lying down the long way, in the spooning-in-front-of-a-movie way, in the head-to-toe lying with a pair of lamps burning and a pair of people reading, it fits me and it fits another—it fits her—really well.

44. She is gone. She is gone, and she will be surprised that I am alive to write this—because she, and everyone who knows me, didn't think I'd survive it. That I can't be alone for a minute. That I can't manage a second of silence. A second of peace. That to breathe, I need a second set of lungs by my side. And to have a feeling? An emotion? No one in my family will show one. Love, yes. Oh, we're Jews, after all. There's tons of loving and complimenting, tons of kissing and hugging. But I mean any of us, any of my blood, to sit and face reality, to sit alone on a couch without a partner and to think the truth and feel the truth, it cannot be done. I sure can't do it. And she knew I couldn't do it. And that's why it ended.

45. It ended because another person wants you to need to be with them, with her, specific—not because you're afraid to be alone.

46. My grandmother had one job in her life. She worked as a bookkeeper at a furniture store for a month before my grandfather proposed. The owner proposed first. She turned the owner down.

47. She had another job. I thought it was her job, and I put it here because I put this scene into every story I write. I lay it into every setting, attribute it to every character. It's a moment that I add to every life I draw, and then cut—for it contains no meaning beyond its meaning to me. It comes from my grandmother and her Mr. Lincoln roses, my grandmother collecting Japanese beetles in the yard. She'd pick the beetles off the leaves and put them in a mason jar to die. And I'd help her. And I'd get a penny for every beetle, because, she told me, she got a penny for every beetle from my grandfather. I believed, until I was an adult, that this was her job. A penny a beetle during rose-growing season.

48. About sacks of corn and the one time I felt like a man: My grandfather and I drive out to the farm stand. It's open, but no one's in it. There's a coffee tin filled with money, under a sign that says SELF-SERVE. Folks are supposed to weigh things themselves and leave money themselves and, when needed, make change. This is how the owner runs it when she's short-staffed. We've come out for corn, and the pickings are slim, and that's when the lady pulls up in her truck. She gets out, makes her greetings, and drops the gate on the back. And in the way industrious folks function, she's hauling out burlap sacks before a full minute has passed. My grandfather says to me, "Get up there. Give a hand."

49. I hop up into the bed of the truck and I toss those sacks of corn down. It's just the thing an able young man is supposed to do—and I'd never, ever have known. But I don't hesitate. I empty the whole thing with her, feeling quiet and strong.

50. They are sacks of Silver Queen and Butter & Sugar, the sweetest corn in the world. She tells us to take what we want, but my grandfather will have no such thing. We fill a paper sack to overflowing and pay our money. At my grandparents', I shuck corn on the back steps, the empty beetle jar tucked in the bushes beside me and music from the transistor coming through the screen of the porch. And—suburban boy, Jewish boy—I've never felt like I had greater purpose, never so much felt like an American man.

51. The woman I love, the Bosnian, she is not Jewish. All the years I am with her, to my family, it's as if she is not. My family so good at it now. My family so masterful. It's not only the past that can be altered and forgotten and lost to the world. It's real time now. It's streaming. The present can be undone, too.

52. And I still love her. *I love you, Bean. (And even now, I don't say it straight. Let me try one more time:* I love you, Bean. *I say it.)* And I place this in the middle of a short story in the midst of our modern YouTube, iTunes, plugged-in lives. I might as well tell her right here. No one's looking; no one's listening. There can't be any place better to hide in plain sight.

53. On Thanksgiving, this very one, I am hunting for a gravy boat in the attic. I find the gravy boat and my karate uniform (green belt, brown stripe) and a shoe box marked DRESSER. Lifting the lid, I understand: It's the remains of my grandfather's towering chest of drawers—a life compacted, sifted down. Inside, folded up, is a child's drawing. It's of a man on a chair, a hat, two arms, two legs—but one of those legs sticks straight out to the side, as if the man were trying to salute with it. The leg at a ridiculous and impossible angle. It's my mother's drawing. She hasn't seen it in years. She doesn't remember filling that box.

54. The drawing is of Great-Grandpa Paul. "Hit by a train," she says. And already—in a loving, not-at-all-angry, Jewish son's way, I'm absolutely furious. She knows I'm writing this story, knows I want to know everything, and here, Great-Grandpa Paul, a lifetime at the railroad and killed by a train. I can't believe it—cannot believe her.

"Oh, no, no," she says, "not killed, not at all. Eighteen when it happened. He survived it just fine. Only, the leg. He could never bend that leg again."

55. The first time Bean brings me home, we walk to the river in Williamsburg. We stand next to a decrepit old factory on an industrial block and stare at Manhattan hanging low across the water, a moon of a city at its fullest and brightest.

56. Bean takes out a key. Behind a metal door is a factory floor with no trace of the business that was. The cavernous space is now a warren of rooms, individual structures, like a shantytown sprouting up inside a box. "I've got a lot of roommates," she says. And then: "I only just finished building. The guys helped me put the ceiling on last night." Toward the back, behind a mountain of bicycle parts, is a grouping of tiny rooms with a ladder (which we climb) leading to a sort of cube on top. She's bracketed together scavenged frames of all shapes and sizes to make four window walls under a window ceiling through which one may stare at the rough beams above. It's a miracle of a room, a puzzle complete. "I guess I'll need curtains now," she says as we sit on her bed. And I say, "You live in a house made of windows, but"—and I motion—"you can't see outside." She takes it well, and takes my hand.

57. I mention him to my grandfather just once. Visiting from college, drinking whiskeys, playing gin. I mention his dead brother Bennie—the army brother—who I'd just found out existed. I say something awkward about the only guy at school called up for the first Iraq war—the good one. I say something about younger brothers, being a younger brother myself.

58. My grandfather picks a card, arranges his hand—making sets. "For a while we owned a building. Two stories. We were landlords to a deli on the ground floor and a pair of tiny apartments upstairs. More than once," he says, "I found a body. I'd head over to check on things before work, and I'd find them. One time in the stairwell, and another, a stiff in the alley, still wearing his hat. These weren't crimes of passion, either. These were deals settled, people done in." He lays his cards facedown on the table. I look at their backs. "Gin," he says. And he goes out to the porch to smoke a cigar.

59. I use the Freedom of Information Act to get at it. We don't have such a law in my family, but the government, the government will tell you things about a missing brother. The government will sometimes share secrets if you ask.

60. Where is my Bean when I need her? Where is Bean when I'm having a feeling I can't face? It's not that I want to share it. It's the exact opposite—the old me in play. What I want is to turn pale for her, saying nothing. I want to go anxious and ask her—should anyone call—to come find me under the bed.

Where she is right then is out dancing on tables. That's what I see in my head. And that's our standard joke during the rare times we speak. Me saying, "I picture you out dancing on tables whenever I wonder what you're up to." "Oh, yeah," she says, "that's me. Out dancing every night."

61. The letter is real—in both realms real. There is an envelope from the government, a pack of papers, forms typed uneven, faded reproductions, large spaces for the clipped explanation. In it is a letter written in my grandfather's hand. It's a beautiful, intelligent, confident (but not cocky) script. It's a polite letter to the government, a crisp, clean letter. He is writing on behalf of his mother, about her son—his brother, killed in (after) the war. They'd filled out the forms, and they'd still not received—he was wondering when they might get—his dead brother's things.

His effects.

Bennie's worldly effects.

62. Here is me, fictionalized, sitting on the couch with a letter, written in my grandfather's hand. I am weeping. I don't know if I've ever seen his handwriting before. I think to call my mother, to tell her what I'm holding. I think to call my brother, or maybe Cousin Jack. But really, more than anyone, I think to call that missing love—that missing lover. Because it's her I wish were with me; it's her I want to share it with right now. And more so, to find myself weeping from a real sadness—not anxious, not disappointed, not frustrated or confused—just weeping from the truth of it, and the heartbreak of it, and recognizing it as the purest emotion I've ever had. It's this I want to tell her, that I'm feeling a pure feeling, maybe my first true feeling, and for this—I admit it—I am proud.

63. I am sad for my grandfather, ten years passed, and his mother, dead forty, and his brother, sixty years gone from this world. I am on the couch alone, and I am weeping. It is the purity of the letter, the simplicity of it: Your last brother dead, and you're asking for his things.

Camp Sundown

I want I should talk to Rabbi Himmelman."

This from Agnes Brown, seventy-six years old, standing behind Josh's chair in the dining hall and addressing the back of his head.

Josh turns to her. She is not alone. She is never alone—Arnie Levine, seventy-eight, is at her side. "You both know," Josh says, "Rabbi Himmelman is gone. I am the director—I've been the director all summer."

"You're too young to be the director," Arnie says, her defender.

"And you, Arnie, are too old to be at camp."

"It's Elderhostel," Agnes says.

"Is there instructional swim?"

"We can," Agnes says, "have a swim lesson in the lake."

"Any place with instructional swim," Josh says, definitive, "is camp."

He holds her gaze, staring eye to eye, though he sits and she stands. She is shrinking, his Agnes. Every summer, the old people grow smaller as the children grow big. Josh has decided that there is only so much height in the world and the inches must change hands.

He turns back to his lunch in time to see it carried off by one of the girls brought in from Poland to do the kitchen work. They are good workers, the Polish girls. And they are paid a fair wage. Though it is, Josh feels, a woeful way to see America—or not see it—these young women ferried straight to the Berkshires to care for Jews too young or too old to care for themselves.

By the time Josh is finished thinking this thought, his lunch, and the Polish girl, have disappeared into the kitchen. He grabs hold of his coffee mug and clasps it tight. He can sense the pair still hovering at his back.

It is always like this with the campers from this side of the lake. They are very old, some of them. They are very slow. Sometimes very sick. And yet, wherever Josh goes, however fast, however far, he can feel them right behind.

Arnie's stiff, speckled hand is at his shoulder, tapping, Agnes talking.

"Boychik," she says, "Squirt. What has happened to Himmelman? Always he takes care."

"Why do you talk like that?" Josh says.

"Like what?"

"Like 'Always he takes care.' Like you haven't been in Livingston, New Jersey, for the last fifty years. Like it's not now 1999, the cusp of a new millennium. Honestly, where does it come from, the 'I want I should talk to the rabbi' and all that?"

"Rude boy!" she says. "Still, you are a nice rude." This part she tells to Arnie. "In this way, the emotional ones are disrespectful, because they are afraid to have feelings." Here she turns back to Josh and winks. "My granddaughter, she is rude, too."

"The vegan?" Josh says. "The born-again Hassidic vegan with four kids?"

"Yes," Agnes says. "Maybe you'll meet her. At your point, a bald head"—Josh reaches up to rub what's left of his hair— "and this job—a sad job, you'll admit? For us, a treat, but for you, well, this? Three months a year living in a pressboard house smells like raccoons . . . I'd say, for you a nice divorcée maybe is good. On visiting day, maybe have a stroll, the two of you. Steal a kiss. Maybe let her walk ahead and have yourself a stare at the center of a nice solid tush and ignore in the end how wide."

" 'Tunnel vision,' they call that now," Arnie says, always adding his "now," as if all the others are trapped in the past and only he has access to the present.

"Visiting day," says Josh, holding up a finger to Arnie, another point. "Did you hear her? She said, 'on visiting day'. If it has visiting day, it's camp."

"The lady," Arnie says, "she asked for Himmelman. He was the one who worried on us. Tanglewood, Himmelman always got us a place. And bug spray, always, for free—a can in his pocket. A *schpritz* when you needed. My fifth summer here, and after the first, I never got malaria again."

"You didn't get malaria," Josh says. "We don't have malaria. We have Lyme disease—and you didn't get that. You were just tired."

"Yes, it was the Lyme," he tells Agnes. "That's what I had. They nearly killed me, here." And to Josh: "You still haven't said why a rabbi just disappears—"

"Because it's not your concern, is why. A problem," says Josh. "A problem on the children's side of the camp. All you need to know is, I'm here now, and Himmelman is gone."

"What problem?" Agnes says. "I saw no little boys face-down in the lake. Is it the turtles?"

"No, it's not turtles. Kids—I'll have you know—do not complain about turtles. They love them. They can outrun them. Only old people complain about turtles. And because of that, I've had their habitat moved, poor things. I've had them fished from the lake and moved far, far away."

"They will come back," Arnie says. "Like elephants—that's how the turtles remember."

"And Himmelman?" Agnes says.

For once, Arnie helps Josh out. "When they say, 'a problem'? Today, that means what we used to call a pervert before there were lawyers like squirrels, hundreds waiting in every tree. Back in my day, every church in Brooklyn kept in its icebox, like beer, a six-pack of altar boys. To get enough kids together for a stickball game, my son would have to sit on the stoop and wait for them to thaw—"

"What are you saying?" Agnes says, drawing him back.

"Himmelman—he is a fondler. He fondles. Our friend who got us always tickets." Arnie shakes his head, disappointed. "Terrible to learn. He seemed so nice and always the hands where you could see them, waving while he talked."

"What are you saying?" Agnes says. "Is that Yiddish, *fondul*? I don't understand."

"No, no," Arnie says. "Fondle—*fondle* is to touch. Everything sounds Yiddish to you. Far-fetched, far-flung . . ."

"Farflung *is* Yiddish."

"No," Arnie says, "it's not. Anyway, the boy is saying, this one—too good for your granddaughter because she wears now a wig and eats the snafu hot dogs."

"Tofu," Josh says.

"What he is trying to tell us is that he got a promotion because of a fondle. He's a pervert's replacement. Big shot!"

"Thank you," Josh says. "Anyway, anyone who signed up for tickets to Tanglewood will get tickets. . . . Did you sign up on the sheet?"

"We signed," Arnie says.

"Then it's done," Josh says. "Then you can go hear music."

"Okay," Agnes says.

"Good. Now, if I turn back to the table, if I scooch around

and reach for 'a nice piece of honey cake,' as you'd say, my dear Agnes, will you still be back there?"

"There is one more thing," Agnes says.

"That's what I wanted to know. Tell me, is it the same 'one more thing' as the last two days? Is it the same topic that we promised never to address out loud, and if we really do need to address it, then not in the dining hall, where the subject of said 'one more thing' might hear and might be wounded and might have a really, really rotten time here at . . . at Elderhostel?"

"If you know," Agnes says, "if you want to ask with a long sentence being a teaser and an ironic maker, then why don't you do something?"

It is then that he passes. The big man, Doley Falk—quiet-looking and sweet as sugar. He is not one of the troublemakers who complain all day to Josh, morning to night, for whom life has turned into one unbroken disappointment. He's just a serious old bridge player, come from Toledo, Ohio, who wants nothing more than to eat kosher food and play cards, and to scream "Two no trump!" when he feels the Alzheimer's sneaking his way.

He is one of the campers who offers Josh his moments—the caught moments that make Josh come back every year, that get him through the winters of planning and recruiting, that, in fact, make it not a sad job for a man to have, but make it plain beautiful.

The first year, it was Rita Desberg, staring off at the lake. Josh spotted her standing stock-still as a mist rose and the sun dropped—a moment so peaceful that even her body for an instant forgot the tremor built in. The second summer it was Charlie Kornblum, his life only tragedy, stories too sad to repeat, and there, Josh saw it, so simple. It was Charlie stepping aside and smiling as a tumble of junior campers rolled by, kicking up behind them a wall of dust.

They are few and far between, these precious instants. And big Doley, a new camper here for the last two weeks of summer, is one to offer them. Josh has already seen.

Doley Falk does not smile at children. He does not stare at the lake. He takes no joy in eating, and snaps his paper when the widows take the chair by his side. But when that hulk of a man sits down at a bridge table, when he hears the first ruffle of the deck, he nods to his partner and looks, positively, like he's eighteen again, a sparkle in his eye.

He's a joy to watch. A pure affirmation of why Josh does what he does. He is one of Josh's specials, and he won't have the man's time here besmirched. But Agnes, she won't leave off him. She and Arnie won't let the man be.

"I'm telling you with respect," Josh says. "The camplike structure, for good and for bad, it revives certain adolescent elements of human nature. You come every year, you two. You stay the whole summer. And you cannot help it. When it comes to the two-weekers, the newbies, the last-session bridge players—toward them, you are, inevitably, cruel." He raises a hand, not rudely, just to stop them from speaking. "*I'm sorry, but it's true.* You always cold-shoulder them—I see what you do. And forgive me for saying it, but you treat them like the new kids in high school bused in for ninth grade."

Arnie brings out the big guns. He rolls up a sleeve and flashes the number on his arm.

"I wouldn't know from ninth grade. Never went. But camp? My share of camps. A different camp than this one, yes? You want camps? I know camps. I know from human nature. And I have seen before. I know—"

"I'm sorry, I'm sorry," Josh says too loudly. "What can I say to numbers? My apologies. On the matter of camps, I defer."

Arnie comes in close. "You don't see what we see," he says.

"Maybe at the cash machine, the code to get money is gone from my head. Maybe sometimes my own grandchildren, I admit it—their names can't be found. But the faces from back then, from that place," Arnie says.

And Agnes, with vigor: "These, we do not forget."

"Leave him be!" Josh says. He is almost yelling, which he never does. They are old. They talk a lot. They push buttons. They have lost the sense, or the will, to self-edit. They enjoy the privileges of old age. He does not get frustrated, but this, this accusation—it is more than mean, and more than confused; it is beyond the glimmers of dementia that make themselves constantly known.

"Don't tell me you can't see it," Agnes says. "When he sits down at that bridge table, that face, it turns to what it was. It turns back into the face of—"

"Beautiful!" Josh yells. "*Beautiful!* The man looks beautiful when he plays!"

And now it's not just Doley Falk who turns to look at Josh. It's the whole room that's staring. Because somehow Josh is standing, and somehow he is screaming, and somehow tiny, sweet, maddening Agnes is holding up a shaky hand in front of her, as if, as if . . . His Agnes looks afraid. She steps back, teetering as if she might fall. And Josh steps forward, reaching. When she is steadied, he says, "Enough. It's time to leave that nice man alone."

"Go shit in a lake," Arnie says to him, and walks off holding Agnes's hand.

. . .

Josh rushes out into the heat, out of the air-conditioned meat locker that the old folks like for a dining hall. He rushes out, shaking, into the sun. Seven years at the camp, six as assistant director, and never has he raised his voice, not once. Not to the aged.

He heads for the path to the kids' side of the lake. A little fresh air, a little youthful energy. He needs it to calm down. But he simply cannot—he cannot have them saying it. It is madness. He cannot let Agnes and Arnie infect the whole place.

Doley Falk, they think, was there with them—back in those other camps. They are convinced Doley Falk is a murderer. Agnes remembers him positioned at a fence. She remembers him, a Nazi camp guard. A Demjanjuk.

Now Josh is not saying forget. But this idea . . . Doley Falk, a Nazi. An old Nazi hiding in the Berkshires under the guise of a blue-toed low-sodium bridge-playing Jew. It is madness. It is too much to take.

Josh stays by the lake on the kids' side until he is feeling nearly copacetic, at the edge of true peace. That is precisely when he finds himself—with all that open space—cornered by Lou Lebovick, head of Youth Sports.

"We got issues here, too," Lou says. "It's like you only come over when one of the old folks needs a spare part. Is that what you're after? A fresh kidney? A nice free-range, kosher-fed, Horace Mann–educated heart? I tell you, they pump like the dickens inside the little ones. It's a wonder their heads don't pop off from the pressure."

Josh steps back to study Lou. And he can't help it. He hears Agnes talking inside his head. *A thirty-six-year-old man who unwinds tetherballs for a living—this is a life?* It fills Josh with pity, and he hooks arms with Lou and walks him to the very edge of the water so that their sneakers take root in the mud. Josh points across the lake to a structure, and Lou's eyes follow in a squint. "That is my office over there, and my cabin behind it, both of which you know. The doors are forever open to you, Lou, as they always have been. Canoes, paddles, fresh T-balls and tees—honestly, when have you ever wanted for something?"

"I know," Lou says, looking sheepish.

"So tell me? What is it? Basketballs? Basketball pumps? What is it that I can do?"

"Needles," Lou says. "The needles that go between the pumps and the balls."

. . .

Josh's office door is indeed perpetually open. To Lou Lebovick. To Agnes. To the Polish girls. To anyone with any problem at all. Because of this, the air conditioner stays off—a waste. And because the old folks, at the best of times, can't hear anything Josh is saying, he's also forced to avoid the whir of a fan. This leaves the office sweltering, a nice touch that Josh appreciates, for people visit to complain, but no one dares stay long.

First thing the next morning, it is the Blachors, Yama and David. They've come all the way from Santa Fe to play bridge for two weeks, their first time. The Blachors live in an adobe house, they tell him. They retired from Englewood, New Jersey, to live in an adobe house because they'd heard too many terrible stories over the years. It is very dangerous to sleep in a house made of wood. It's very easy for them to catch fire. And this pair, twenty years gone from the East Coast, has discovered they can no longer bear to sleep in anything like a rustic wooden cabin. They cannot bear being seated too deeply in that firetrap of a dining hall. And they have taken to wearing, each, around their necks, a smoke alarm on a lanyard woven specifically for this purpose in crafts.

"You cannot wear those contraptions," Josh tells them.

"They sow panic. They convince the others that there is a danger. And certain ideas in a closed environment are contagious," Josh says, "like fire." To which the Blachors, nodding, recoil. "All the wood in the camp," he says, "the walls, the floors, the dock—it's fire retardant. The rooms are already equipped with detectors. In the dining hall, it's the same. If anything on the grounds so much as warms up, I will hear the alarm, the fire department will hear, remotely—"

"Up here? The fire department? Do you have any idea how many miles it lies distant?" Yama asks.

"How many miles does it lie distant?" Josh says.

"Twelve," David tells him. "Twelve miles of curvy road. Of barely a two-lane road. That is how far away help rests."

"Well, you decide how to proceed," Josh tells them. "You can wear them, but not to activities, not to anywhere where anyone else will see. I'll have your meals brought to your room, if need be. I'll have a deck of cards sent over. If you insist on wearing the smoke detectors, you're stuck in your room playing gin."

The Blachors consider, and as they do, Josh can see from a hundred yards away the mountain that is Doley Falk rushing his way, the mountain coming to the man. Doley holds a hand to his chest, his face red, a sweat on him. He's in obvious distress and headed straight for Josh's open office door.

To the Blachors, Josh says, "How about this? You go right now, and for today you can wear them—but no testing. I don't want to hear them. Today, you can wear them under a nice light sweater. Tomorrow, we reconvene."

And the Blachors, feeling successful, are gone.

Josh pulls a water from his minifridge and an ice pack from its freezer. He is always thinking ahead about disaster. A perfect first summer. He wants no ambulances, no paramedics. He wants no blown hearts on this side of the camp, and no

Himmelmans trolling the other—he won't have it, not on his watch. Josh will send every single camper home, healthier and happier than when he or she arrived.

Doley is at his door.

"They say to me 'Hi'" is what Doley keeps repeating, sounding delirious, while Josh tries to ease this giant man into a chair, to get him to sit, to drink, to cool. Josh drops the ice pack to the floor and, without asking, pours the cold water on Doley's head.

Doley calms. He says, "Thank you," and, still panting, begins again. "They say to me 'Hi,' and I say to them 'Hi,' because I think they say to me 'Hi' and wave. . . . But they are not. It is *heil*. They are saying to me *'Heil,'* to a Ukranian Jew, who has been. And the waving, the arms up in the air, they are not—"

"Is it Arnie?" Josh says. "Arnie and Agnes?"

"Names, I don't know," Doley says, panting, and now unable to get his breath. He holds one hand low, approximating height, and the other yet lower, right near to the floor.

"Yes," Josh says, grabbing for another bottle, this time pouring water on himself. He is afire, afire with anger, enough to set to ringing the alarms hung around the Blachors' necks. Josh fans Doley with the camp songbook. "You don't worry," he whispers, practically cooing. "I'll take care of it. I know exactly who."

. . .

Josh is losing control of the camp. His first year in charge and, so close to the end of the summer, he's losing the reins. Josh storms into the reading group, where eight of the oldsters sit in a circle, clutching large-type editions of *Les Misérables* before them. A retired fifth-grade teacher who summers in

Lexington has driven up in a chocolate Lexus sports coupe to lead the weekly class. She is dressed, head to toe, in summer Chanel.

"I don't know why they call this book *Les Misérables*," she says, leaning into the circle, as if sharing a secret. "As you will discover, this book is not less miserable. It is *more* miserable than you can imagine." Josh points at Agnes and Arnie, interrupting, and, like a principal, he says, "You two, in my office right now."

Arnie and Agnes cross their arms, defiant.

"We don't go!" Agnes says. "Whatever you need, you tell us here. We are all one," she says of the assembled campers. "The secrets we know, they know—and agree."

"They agree?" Josh says.

"They agree," Arnie says.

The teacher gives a series of nervous pats to a hive of Aqua Net–frozen hair. "What do we all agree on?" she says, trying to stay in charge of her domain, exactly as Josh is trying to do with his. "What is it we know?"

"It's all right," Josh says to her, a forced smile. "You can go. Class dismissed, or whatever it is. There's an emergency today—a disciplinary matter."

"But I drove all this way from Lexington. I could have been with my boys by the pool. I've got a lesson plan, already set."

"Then you're fired," Josh says, "if that makes it easier."

"Fired?" she says. "I volunteer."

"Then unvolunteer. It's an emergency, I'm begging you. Please, get out of the room." As she leaves, looking mortally offended, he says to the others, "And any of you who disagree with this madness, who understand it as such, feel free to go to the canteen. My treat, whatever you want, put it on my tab."

The others, like Agnes and Arnie, cross their arms.

"You really want to throw your lot in with these two?" Josh says. "They're in hot water, I tell you. Up to their necks in it."

The others nod, accepting.

"We boil together," Arnie says.

"You boil?" Josh says. "Really?" He cannot believe this. "No," he yells. "No, you don't boil. I don't give you that option. All of this stops right now. You leave that man alone. He is no murderer. He is no Nazi. You are—all of you—mistaken."

"How can we be mistaken," Arnie asks, "if Agnes is not mistaken?"

Josh looks to Agnes, trying out sentences in his head, wanting to be nice. "You are convinced that you're right," he says to her. "But it is time, it is memory, that has turned you wrong."

"Those faces," Agnes says; "time can't see them undone."

Josh is nodding. Josh is looking empathic, preparing to speak with his "master's in social work" tone. He will delicately and apologetically disabuse Agnes of this notion. But Arnie will not have it.

"No," Arnie says. "Do not go and dress up disrespect in the clothes of compassion. I can tell," he says, wagging a finger. "You think we don't feel the creak in every thought, same as to the bend in our knees? You think we do not, like the archer—"

"The archer?" Josh says.

"Yes, with the arrows. The archer, absolutely. They adjust for the wind. This, with every word, we do, measuring before we speak. We know we are old. We know what is lost and what is left. But certain faces cannot be unseen. No more than those little *pishers* on the other side of the lake, with their winkles touched by the rabbi—no more than they will ever wake to a morning where they don't first see Himmelman when they open their eyes. Mercy on those boys."

"Wrong!" Josh yells. "Whisperings! And forget now Himmelman!" he yells, his diction ruined by this place.

"Because you forget Himmelman," Arnie says, "because some board decides to forget Himmelman, because it is better for the camp to forget, it does not mean justice wants to see Himmelman forgotten. Such actions are not in the service of justice, Herr Direktor. And for us, for the Book Group Eight—"

"You're the Book Group Eight now?" Josh asks, incredulous.

"It was either that," Agnes says, "or 'the Miserables.' But the novel, we haven't yet read."

"Our name, yes!" Arnie says, "And our manifesto: We will not leave Doley Falk among us, to bid out, at the bridge table, his last days."

"Then call the police on him if he's so guilty," Josh says. "Twelve miles away," he says, now quoting the Blachors. "They'll be here in no time. Share your manifesto with them."

"You think we are lawless, Herr Direktor? This is the first thing we tried, those local yokels."

"And?"

"And they won't come. They mocked. They said to try Interpol, to call up Her Majesty's Secret Service and ask for James Bond. They said they don't do Nazi hunting anymore. They said the kids at this camp ordered twenty-five pizzas to the station last year, and the year before, too. Prank calls. Nonsense calls. And they say every weekend they need to bring back underage counselors from town, each one drunk as a skunk."

"So, you see?" Josh says. "These are professionals, men of the law, and even over the phone they grasp how crazy a notion this is. They, who are sworn to follow up on these matters, know it's best to ignore it. So tell me, what would you like us to do here at camp? What could you possibly want me to do better?"

"A trial. A camp trial. A jury of his peers. If he is innocent, we leave him be."

"And if he's guilty?" Josh says, smiling, proud of himself. "What punishment could a sleepaway camp possibly give?"

"Don't you understand?" Agnes says. "If he's guilty, then he's your Nazi, too."

Josh ponders this. At first, he feels sick at the notion. What if there's real guilt? And then he turns, angry, ludicrous as the notion is. "But he's not guilty. He isn't. And there'll be no trial."

"A shame, then," Arnie says, actually sounding threatening, "because either way, justice must be served."

.   .   .

Josh opens his eyes to the Blachors, Yama and David, standing over his bed. "Outside," they say. "A fire."

His mind and body awake in different measure, Josh pauses only to zip his shorts and grab the emergency walkie-talkie from its charger by the door. He's outside faster than he's ever been in his life, and, jumping from the porch, still airborne, he calls for the Blachors to tell him the way. "The quad," they say. "Our cabins." And Josh races over at great speed.

What Josh finds there is not really a fire. What it is, is *yahrzeit* candles, hundreds of them, stolen from the supply closet, memorial candles in their jam jars lit and dropped into paper day-trip lunch bags. A whole night's work spread out before him, the bags lined up, it seems, to form a giant Jewish star.

It takes Josh a moment, his system flushed through with adrenaline, his brain primed and in emergency mode. It takes an extra beat to understand what this installation is. *Who* it is. Then Josh gets it. Arnie and Agnes. Symbols flipped. It is their burning cross.

The other old people, thank God, have no idea. At this point, they're nearly all out of their cabins, enjoying the spectacle. They take it as a sweet, sanctioned nighttime activity. The songbooks are already open, and the younger campers in pajamas, their sneakers unlaced, stream across the path from the other side of the lake to join in the fun. They will sing and dance for the old people, earning points for a mitzvah project, good deeds that will be repaid in Italian ices and soda. The counselors, excited themselves, have begun to build a bonfire.

Josh hunts down Doley, frantic, terrified that he, too, has sussed out what this burning star is. As the bonfire comes up, as the first hint of real smoke blends with the air of a perfect piney foothills night, Josh finds that giant man at the side of his cabin in the shadows, and he can see that Doley understands. Doley looks afraid, and—Josh hates himself for thinking it, the power of suggestion—he looks guilty, too: guilty, cowed, and afraid. Josh accepts then that he is losing his mind. As he runs off to hunt for those book-group hooligans, he wishes he could call the old director. He knows Himmelman would ask him to repeat it twice. "Vigilante Nazi justice," Josh would say. "Retribution and recrimination. Geriatric revenge."

Josh's face is a one-man mask of comedy and tragedy. His scowl is in constant rotation with a big fat smile as he searches out Agnes and Arnie. He grins and slaps counselors on the back, making the most out of what is, hands down, the summer's most successful cross-generational event, and then he relocks his jaw, renarrows his eyes, and maneuvers toward his prey.

Josh circles and circles without finding even one of the Book Group Eight, a damning absence. He loiters by the bonfire, busying himself with policing all the tiny pyromaniacs who draw too close to the flames. Livid, he waits.

It's there that Agnes and Arnie choose to appear. They edge out of the darkness toward Josh, stepping into the halo of firelight.

"Is this you two?" Josh says, his rage unchecked. "Is this the work of the Miserable Eight?"

"Who's to know?" Agnes says. "At our age, who even remembers what happened a minute before?"

"She's making you your own point, *boychik*," Arnie says.

"I get that," Josh says.

Arnie is looking pleased. "Now how does it sound?"

"Is everything a joke with you two? This is a witch-hunt. It's harassment. Is that really your idea of justice? You've got an old man, who's been through who knows what in life, standing off in the shadows, afraid."

"Let him know from some fear," Agnes says. "Let him know worse."

"No," Josh says. "It ends now."

"It ends when there's action," Arnie says. "You take it, or we take it. That's how it stops."

"You want action from me?" Josh says. "You really want that? Fine, then. Here . . . here is action."

Arnie and Agnes watch as the director runs off, his own sneakers unlaced like the children's. He races into the library at a gallop. Seconds later, he bursts back out the open door, his arms impossibly full, books and videos dropping as he charges their way.

"No more Movie Mondays," he screams, dropping his pile at Agnes's and Arnies's feet. And then, one after the other, he begins throwing books and videotapes into the fire. "*Marathon Man, Boys from Brazil, Three Days of the Condor, Parallax View.*

I'm telling you," he screams, "every paranoid Nazi favorite, every Ira Levin. I will leave you nothing but *Grumpy Old Men* and *California Suite*."

Josh stops only when he hears the young people laughing at him, enthralled with his tantrum. And from the old people, the opposite reaction: They are frozen, slack-jawed.

"What?" Josh screams. "What?"

They do not answer. And when their gazes shift, Josh's gaze shifts with them back toward the library. It is one of the Polish girls coming up behind him. She has busied herself picking up the books he dropped. And now, stern-faced, a good helper, she tosses them into the flames from a distance, one after the other. In the firelight, the thrown books flutter, open-paged, like swallows. Josh watches the girl, like seeing a shadow of himself.

Agnes is at Josh's ear. "A book-burning. This, we never thought we'd see again."

Josh turns to her, his voice high, his eyes brimming and casting back the blaze. "I'm only destroying the ones that incite."

Arnie cackles at that. He is the only one of the old people laughing. "It is not those movies that get into our heads," he says. "It is our heads that get into those movies. It is precisely because of history that such horrible things get thought."

. . .

The camp director's table in the dining hall is like the captain's table a ship. It is a coveted place to be invited to eat, and Rabbi Himmelman had kept it full every meal, a mix of seniors and kids ferried over from the other side of the lake. Josh favors his meals alone, his only time to be at peace and think. And he knew, all summer long, that he was being judged for this lapse. Well, Josh is fixing that now, fixing it with Doley Falk.

He invites him, along with his bridge partner, Shelley Nevins, to sit at his side. He does this for lunch, and then at dinner. To show leadership. To mend fences. But he can feel, oppressive, the eyes of those eight. They sit at one table now. And Arnie and Agnes no longer approach Josh with their requests. It is, Josh knows, now his job to approach them. Josh has lost the reins.

He does this during dessert course, when young and old alike are most distracted.

"Please," Josh says in a loud whisper to Agnes and Arnie and the rest of their group. "It was a nice event in the end, okay? But what you did last night—"

"A big hit!" Arnie says.

"Yes, I've only just acknowledged it," Josh says, mustering deference. "Still, the intent behind it . . . I don't want to call the police for real."

"Who, on us?" Agnes says. "On us—over him? Go ahead," she says. "Knock yourself out. I'll break rocks for the rest of my days."

"They don't break rocks anymore," Arnie says. "No more license plates, either. Now it's kid gloves, and high school diplomas."

"Nobody's going to jail," Josh says. "Not yet. That's what I want to avoid."

"Someone needs jail," Agnes says. "The fat man needs jail."

"Let me start again. Let me say it this way. How many nights are left this year? How many days to go?"

"Two more nights," one of the eight answers.

"Exactly. Two. Can we not make it that long? I'll give you my word. Swear to you—"

"Jews don't swear," Agnes says. "Forbidden."

"Then promise. I give you my promise. You give me two

days, and you'll never see him again. I won't have him back—even if he applies and sends a check."

"Not good enough," Arnie says. "Blindness. Ignoring. These things will not do."

"What if," Josh says, "what if I also accept some of what you say? What if we take that route?"

"Go on," Agnes says. And with her "Go on," the eight seated at the table lean back and face him with a mix of cocked eyebrows and jutting chins, readying themselves for his pitch.

"What if I admit," Josh says, "that it's possible? . . . No, not possible . . . What if I say that you're right? And that maybe the man was there, a guard, in a camp, watching. Can we accept as a group that maybe he witnessed some things—that he took part, but *only* as a witness—and that if he was there doing nothing but watching, that maybe, at this point, around the world, all these years later, that maybe that's the same as nothing at all?" They listen; they consider; they stare.

It's Arnie who speaks.

"To murder is to murder. To stand by for a murder is to murder. To hide the history of murder is to murder. The turning away of the head is the same as turning the knife. If Doley was there," Arnie says, "he should swing like Eichmann from the rope."

"Not so," Josh says.

Arnie shakes his head. "To watch and say nothing, it is as bad as the killing."

"Do you really think that?" Josh says. "Someone is a murderer even if he never laid a hand on a soul?"

"Guilty is the watcher," Agnes says. "Guilty, all."

.   .   .

That night, Josh again opens his eyes to the Blachors. This time, they hover above him, a dream. Josh screams silently, his mouth twisted up. He pulls wildly at the covers, trying to hide from the floating couple, their smoke detectors no longer detectors, but lenses fitted to their chests. Josh had read an article, seen a terrifying picture of a cow's four-chambered stomach at work, a ruminating window patched into its side. It is this same setup in the dream, but the windows are set into the Blachors' chests. And through each of those portholes, where the heart would go, Josh sees a giant solid-gold Jewish tooth beating. Josh stares at them: grotesque stolen artifacts patched up to leaky ventricles—those horrible teeth beating like bloody gold hearts. All the while, he pulls at the covers, whimpering, but the covers, as if carved of stone, won't move.

Josh wakes unsettled, unable to believe all is all right. He decides to walk the inner perimeter of the camp to make sure his charges are silent and safe. Josh opens his cabin door to scattered garbage, to a pair of raccoons, masked thieves, tumbling off his porch and ambling fatly away. Josh puts a hiking lamp on his head and walks off behind them. And he thinks, because of his terrible dream, that the light is his own lens to a shiny gold-tooth brain.

The old folks' side is perfectly silent, peaceful. Happy to discover this, starting to relax into the night, he drifts on over to the path around the lake. That is when he sees it, on the far side, the shapes moving, splashing around. He turns off his light, he listens to the silence, and now, using the moon, he walks.

.   .   .

What Josh sees (and it's not the first time this summer) is a forbidden night swim. It's off at the far end of the lake, by the wooded dogleg that edges up to the deep. Josh waits until he's closer to scream, "Kids! Out! And clothes back on." There is scurrying, and splashing, and the usual signs of feeble escape. He sees a defiant one, maybe the head of swim staff, still float-ing, not even trying to get away. "Charidan!" Josh calls. "I will dock you! I will dock your pay! This kind of example, for the kids!" he calls. And Charidan goes under the water, so that only one head remains bobbing nearby. "That's right, stay under!" Josh calls. "That's where you'll find your check!" And he keeps calling, keeps threatening, keeps chiding as he moves closer. He does this to feel less alone in the night as he approaches, and he does this to give himself one more moment in the life that was, before accepting what surely woke him. It wasn't the *scritch-scratch* of raccoon nails on his porch, or the blood of a gold-hearted dream. What drew him from bed, Josh knows, was the feel of a threat ignored too long. What pulled him to the lake was dear Doley Falk, in the midst of sinking. It was eight aged campers depositing their dead.

The water is calm at the spot where he'd seen the body floating. The only ripple left to the lake is around Arnie, his head submerged to his eyes, and coming up, guppy-mouthed, for gasps of air.

The others are barely hidden, shivering behind a thicket of trees. Josh, going to speak, says, "How did you move him?" surprised to hear this as the question that escapes from his mouth.

"He walks," Agnes says, "now he does not walk."

"Self-transporting," Arnie says, forever the explainer.

"Oh my God," Josh says. "Please, tell me this is another loop in the dream. Please wake me, sweet Agnes," Josh says. "Come up out of the water, Arnie. Tap me on the shoul-der. Wake me with that stiff murdering hand." It is a light tone that Josh uses, the way he used to talk to them before things turned bad.

"We can't wake you," Agnes says. "It is, all of it, real."

"But, a murder?"

"This is what happens when you fence people in," Arnie says. "This is always true, and never changes. A rule. A camp is a camp, Herr Direktor. Inside, different kinds of justice will form."

Josh looks from face to face, and each one, sure, holds his gaze.

"What do we do?" he says, beginning to panic.

"You can call the police if you want," Arnie says. "Twelve miles, you said. If anyone is awake, they can be here, fifteen minutes. With sirens, maybe less."

"Oh my God!" Josh yells again. "Oh my Lord, what have you done?"

"This," Agnes says, "you already know."

Arnie moves toward the shallows, rising from the water, a frail, brittle-boned man. "It's not anymore what have we done," he says. "It's, what will you do? That's the question. It's you who gets to decide the end of our lives, and the end of your camp. It's you who gets to choose if this moment is remembered at all."

"But I don't," Josh says. "You have decided already."

"We have decided one thing. You decide the rest. You can make it go away if you want, same as with the rabbi. Like Himmelman disappears, dirty fondler, without a trace. That crime your board can swallow? Then let them swallow this—justice served. A ravage avenged. Put this on your list of crimes."

"Even if I'd want to," Josh says. "Even if that would be right—"

"Simple boy," Agnes says. "Naïve boy."

"Tell them," Arnie says, "the police, the family, the world.

A thousand pills a day between us. Tell them what, about us, they already think. Tell them Alzheimer's, tell them mini-strokes, tell them brain plaque and sundowning. They will put up signs. They will search the woods. But they will understand; all will understand. There will be different kinds of dementia. They will accept that old Mr. Falk was taken over by one. If you help us to sink him down good, trap him in the weeds, in two days, three, the kids already gone, he will come back up. He will rise, an old man confused in pajamas, and no one will think past it twice. Consider the good you do, young Josh. Think of the good of this camp. Think, can all eight of us be so crazy, or is it possible that Agnes is right? It's your choice, Director. You take one crime to bed with you every evening, take a second one tonight."

"What kind of choice is that?" Josh says. "What have you done to this man?"

"To which man?" Agnes asks, honestly confused. "To him," she says, pointing into the lake, "or to you?"

And off to the side, all of them feel it. There is motion. A counselor maybe, a camper, crawling along the ground. Maybe it's already a policeman watching, here to haul Josh and his seniors away. Josh turns on his headlamp, giving it a twist. The light follows his gaze, and this he turns to the stretch of grass between the soaking oldsters hidden in the trees and the soft edge of the lake where Arnie now stands, his feet planted in the mud.

One of the old people says, "Look!" But, again, the light on his head—Josh already sees. Slow and steady, a pair of giant turtles first, and then another trio, slightly smaller, moving slowly behind. They are crossing in front of the thicket where the old people hide. "Like elephants," Arnie says. "That's how the turtles remember."

At this, Arnie steps up onto the grass, and the old

people come closer, moving along with him, to Josh's side. They watch this procession, standing together, murderers all. They watch those turtles on their slow march and behold those ancient creatures, shell-backed and the color of time, as they lower themselves, turtle upon turtle, disappearing into the stillness of the lake.

The Reader

He sits on a box of books in a storage room piled high with such boxes and remembers the old days, as he does every night on the road. A boy by the name of Todd pops in with a cup of coffee. He's younger than the author, everyone so much younger now.

"It's instant," Todd says, handing over the cup. "I hope that's okay. The machine—the barista—it's already shut down."

"Instant's fine," Author says, and takes a sip to prove it.

This night, this is city six or city eight. It is the end of another day of Author's driving around only to find an empty bookshop. Often the stores didn't even have the books that were ordered, let alone an audience to buy them.

Author is not ungrateful. The life he'd led, the writing life, it had been beyond his wildest dreams. He'd been treated generously over the years, touted and well received. Still, Author had put everything he had into this latest novel. Not just emotion, not just all he'd got in the gumption sort of way, but literally *all he had*. All his time, all his money, a hunk of his life. Of course, this is what every book had asked of him, that he forgo all distraction and every comfort, that he simply put his head down and work. But some decades are more delicate than others. And from this one, he'd lifted his eyes up and discovered that he was old.

Author turns around to find Todd still standing there, observing him in his reverie. The boy pulls a handful of creamers from his pocket. He holds the little thimbles out in his palm, reaching right up to Author's chin, as if Author were an old goat at a petting zoo.

"No, thank you," Author says, turning away. "Intolerant," he says, "to lactose—among other things."

. . .

The last time Author read at this store, the barista had not gone home, the staff had not gone home, and the author hadn't drunk coffee. The owner poured whiskey while chasing her starry-eyed workers away. Still, they rushed into the storeroom excitedly to say, "We don't know where to put the people. The audience. They're lined up outside the door."

Tonight there is no one, and Todd peers out into the store one final time to check that it's so. "Let's give it five minutes," he says, unpinning his name tag. Then he takes out a phone and his thumbs start flying.

Author wants to tell the boy certain things. He wants to say, Twelve years. Twelve years on a book—is that now half your life, young man? He wants to tell Todd, One must stand by one's story. It's the same commitment the liar must make, but here it's about sticking by the truth.

In a sudden display of eagerness, Author offers to sign stock.

"Can't return them," Todd says. "The distributors . . . signatures they consider—" And here Todd looks up from texting. He has started a sentence he doesn't want to finish.

"Damaged," Author says, doing it for him. Todd nods. And then the thumbs, they are on the move.

. . .

That you haven't heard of Author—that any recognition you may once have had is beyond recalling—and Author (even in his own estimation) is no longer worth naming, this doesn't take away from what was.

It does not diminish the fine books he wrote. It does not take away from the countless copies bought and read, beloved books, maybe one signed right to you, the volume itself fallen behind your shelves, or your parents', or maybe it is, yes, your grandparents' book—packed away, molding in the basement, the silverfish eating their way through.

At his height, the head of the New York Public Library had waited for Author on the front steps of that venerable institution. A patrician man, the librarian stood rigid in the rain between his two sleeping lions, simply to show respect for Author, coming there to perform.

He then took Author on a tour of the great halls, insistent on exposing him to the wonders of their collection. "This is the cane Virginia Woolf left on the banks of the river when she waded into the waters," the librarian said, "pockets full of stones." He laid this relic in Author's hand for a moment before leading him down below the basin of the old Manhattan reservoir, floor after floor, into the stacks that run deep below Bryant Park. There the librarian turned a giant nickel wheel, parting shelves like the sea, and said, "These are the best sellers of the nineteenth century, where we keep your brothers and sisters, the authors who held your esteemed position one hundred years ago!" Author went to look. Author expected to find the books he cherished from that time.

"Is this . . . ," Author said.

"Yes, yes," said the librarian, beaming. "The giants of the era!"

Author looked again, the spines unfamiliar. *Bloomingdale Row; To the Hills, Boys!; Capshaw Is Rough;* and something with the unfortunate moniker *Scuttle-de-do.* Author's eyes bounced around the shelves, picking up speed until they were near rolling in his head. He fought off a panic. Author had not heard of a one.

"Tastes change," the librarian said. "Isn't it fascinating how much?"

Author had buried the moment away. He'd left it where it sat, deep down below the park. And only now does it come rushing back, all these years later, as Author leaves Todd and the storeroom and his ruined career behind.

Author says thanks to the boy. Author says good-bye. And Todd doesn't understand that this good-bye is not just to him and his store and this town, but it's Author's good-bye to the whole fucking thing.

This last book, Author had typed nearly all of it standing up, fighting an aching back and clacking away at his keyboard with arthritic rope-knuckled fingers. This is how he now worked, the spring gone from his system, bone rubbing against bone.

"If you hit the latch thing, it'll lock behind you" is what Todd yells out from the storeroom. Author hears this as he heads for the front door, thinking that this is what it's come to. The boy in the back on his phone, wholly unconcerned that someone might already be inside loading up on the great treasures of literature and robbing the store. Author skirts the five empty rows of five chairs horseshoed to give the impression of a decent crowd, were they to fill. He keeps his eyes down so as not to see the Staff Choices or Best Sellers, so as not to catch

Reader Favorites or the discount stickers next to the embossed foil prizes awarded to the writers he used to know.

Author is half out that door when he hears a different voice calling. "Author," the voice calls. And then, sharper, more demanding, "Writer," it says. "Writer, you came here to read."

In the empty store, in those empty chairs, sits—invisible until he speaks—one man.

He is small. Much smaller than the author, who is not big. He is also considerably older, which Author thinks must make him at least 110. The man's skin is pale and vitamin-starved. His face hangs loose on his head. Shoved into his mouth like a doorstop is a set of big white teeth that surely sit in a glass by night. The only thing with any life left in it is the hair, boot-polish black. This—Author can't take his eyes off it—it isn't like those choppers. The hair seems real, vibrant, and undyed.

Were Author ever to write again, the hair would be the detail. He'd write of a drawn old man, shrunk inside his clothes, face melting like wax, and this smart, this healthy shock of black hair.

"You came to read," the man says.

"I came to read," Author says.

The man stands there, looking expectant.

Author pretends to misread the cue he is receiving. He feigns impatience. And when the man continues to hold his ground, Author breaks, openly despairing, his voice choked with all the hurt of that night.

"A dozen years," Author says, "day in and day out—writing. Writing all the time. You do not know how many pencils it takes just for the drafting," he says. "Boxes and boxes of pencils. Now look," Author says. "I'm asking you, take a look."

The old man joins the author in surveying the empty room.

"Call it a night, shall we?" Author says. "Yes, let's just call it a career and go home."

The old man, at first invisible himself, now produces a copy of the author's book, which had been invisible in his hand. It is well-worn—in a good way. It looks, in fact, Bible-soft. A hardcover read so much that it curls in his grip.

"There's an investment from me, too," the man says.

"A drink," Author says. "Wouldn't that be better—more personal? Wouldn't you rather—maybe a meal?"

"I'd rather you read. That's what I came for."

They stare at each other. Study faces. And Author, he shakes his head as he hears himself speaking. "Something short," he says, giving in to this ancient man.

"It's not for me to dictate," the old man says. "If it's one word, then one word. The contract—a social contract. It says, If I come, you read."

"It does, doesn't it," Author says, offering a hand and leading the little man to the front row. Author takes a seat himself, angling the chair farther into the horseshoe, and takes up his book to read.

"No," the little man says. "The podium."

"What?"

"The podium."

"We are two," Author says.

The old man looks back, blank.

"As audience," Author says, "you are one." He holds up a finger to illustrate.

"Dignity. A great author."

"I am?"

"You are. A great author. A mighty author. One or one million come to see you, still, from the podium. Read out. Read strong."

And now Author's first impression seems rash. Author no

longer thinks—and he is *ashamed* not to think it, because he knows why he no longer thinks it—that the old man seems so crazy anymore.

Author takes his place at the lectern and opens his book. He gives the same introduction he'd give to one or one million. The same personal, heartfelt warm-up Author used to reserve for the big halls. He remembers a night in Seattle, remembers tripping over the cables running from a TV truck into the theater as he made his way backstage. There, a woman in a headset pulled back the curtain for Author and, for a moment, took hold of his arm. "Remember to raise your eyes to the balcony" is what she'd said. "You can't see, but they're there."

Author reads his heart out for this lone man. He reads so hard, his voice booming, the feel of story-told overtaking him, the rhythm of the sentences running through him, that it puts tears in Author's eyes, tears that he lets fall, so that it is now from memory that he reads, turning the pages while the letters swim.

It's in the midst of this reverie that he does not—for who knows how long—notice Todd standing there, staring back and forth between the author and the man, a strange thump emanating from him. Todd is trying to distract Author, Author thinks, trying to take away from this lovely moment. Why else would this deep bass be coming from him? Author posits that this is maybe some kind of anger radiating off Todd, and then, pulled back to this world, focusing, he understands that the pulse comes from a pair of headphones clamped like hubcaps around Todd's head.

Author, soaring still, reads on.

. . .

Driving in darkness toward the next distant city, Author knows that what he'd just experienced was a gift. Really, how much richer could a writing life be than finding, even for one night, one true reader?

Author rolls this thought around his brain, sucking on it like a sweet-sticky lozenge. He thinks this thought right down to nothing as he barrels along I-80, pulling right at the wheel, his car buffeted by the wind. When the check-engine light pops up, glowing on his dashboard, Author sees it simply as another small test in the life of the true artist. Check engine. Check author. Drive on.

It does not last long, this feeling. It does not last a full twenty-four hours before Author feels ashamed and embarrassed for having driven so far. Author finds himself standing alongside a narrow woman, her wrists girded in copper bangles, as if suited up for some obscure form of war. All Author can think is, Who will she fight in this empty store? Who will even bother to come attacking?

The woman is talking to Author as she lines up a row of tiny point-of-purchase books. "It must be a shock for the once-a-decade novelist," she says. "Startling to see how much things have changed."

"Yes, yes," Author says. "A book every ten years, it's like being a cicada. You spend all that time underground, busy staying alive. And when you finally burrow your way back out, you never know what world you'll find."

The woman waves off the whole situation, and the motion sends the bangles scuttling along her arm, giving off a tinny ring. "Sixteen weeks and three days from now this space belongs to CVS."

Author doesn't know what to say to this, and so he says, "Soap." And then, pointing at his head, "Q-tips." He clears his throat. "Some things will always be in need."

The woman considers, and while she does, Author takes the opportunity to nod in thanks and head for the parking lot door. That's when he hears it. "Author," the voice calls. "Writer. Where do you go?"

Author stops, blinks, an ear cocked toward the room. Author stands with the doorknob in his hand as if he's just heard his own birdcall.

"Writer, always running. A reading tonight!"

Before Author answers, it's the store owner speaking, her voice enough to knock the little man down.

"No reading," she says. "Canceled."

"Canceled why?" the old man says. "Canceled how?"

She looks at him, quizzical. "No one came."

"Someone came," he says. But he's not referring to himself. "The author came. Look right there. Can you see? He holds the door open, letting in the cold."

"Not worth it," the lady says. "No offense, but the time for the reading has come and gone."

"Yes, offense," the old man says. And then he's off rhapsodizing, singing Author's praises. Author does not take it personally. That is, he does not hear the kindnesses as in reference to him. What he hears from this ancient man is a passion for books themselves, from someone bitten by the written word. Author hears what he hears as a fellow reader, and Author remembers.

It was "The Story of My Dovecot." It was Babel, read to him by his mother. She'd sat by the side of his childhood bed and read that story to Author in Russian. This was back in the days when the language whispered at his bedside still held meaning in Author's ears. And look at him now, a lifetime later and he can still see the whole story as if he himself had lived it. For Author, it has remained as vivid as it was upon its first telling, while the Russian was—all of it—gone.

When his mother had finished reading, Author had asked

her if the story was for him. He didn't mean it as metaphor, or exaggeration; he was asking sincerely—a little boy's question—had Mr. Babel composed the story for Author to hear?

His mother, having read him a tale too sad, too dark for a boy so young, had tousled his hair and kissed his head and said, "Of course. Written for you alone, my son." Author, as a child, was amazed and overjoyed and filled with wonder. Somewhere a writer had put something out into the world, and put it out there for Author alone to find. It was an intimacy as real as a friendship.

Author looks over at his reader talking to the bangle-armed woman, cajoling. Here was Author's crackpot. Author's nutcase. And also Author's audience—this ancient, ancient man with his shoe-polish hair and cataracts thick as nails through which he reads. Reads and somehow drives.

The bookstore lady relents, and Author doesn't fight it. He is now truly touched by this man's dedication, here to see him a second night. Author reads his heart out for the old man. And when Author is done, a chastened bookstore lady approaches with a novel that Author humbly signs. It is not for the shop. It's an inscription requested, a book personalized and then returned to its owner. She clasps it to her chest, shielding it behind those bangled arms.

. . .

Author is truly thankful for his champion, his upholder. This is what he tells himself when he finds his one loyal reader wearing a yarmulke and sitting front row at the JCC in St. Paul.

In a yarmulke himself, Author is so grateful for this man who sustains him, who preserves him, who does not turn his back in hard times against him, that the mantra turns into a little prayer. Author recites this from his dais—it comes out of his mouth, a poem. The old man looks thrilled, teeth and hair shining, as he listens to a private devotion that's nearly drowned out by the din of evening-league basketball blowing through a retractable wall. Afterward, he produces a crumpled handwritten schedule with the author's next dates. "Yes, a lovely night, this," the old man says, carefree, perusing.

But every gift and every blessing have a place where they curdle and turn. The man comes to see him at an empty Brookline Booksmith, an empty Three Lives, and an empty Politics and Prose. In Kansas City, when a pair of drunks stumbles in mid-reading to suck up the free wine, Author slams his book shut, only to hear the cry from his audience of one, "Author, read on!"

"Read on," yes, but for how long? Author is a man surviving on memory and the fumes of prestige. He addresses this to his reader—forever at his heels—in a quaint pueblo-inspired bookshop in Alamosa. "This book," Author says, "it's not a novel, it's a tombstone. Why not just hammer it in the ground above my head? My name's already on the front."

"A mistake to make such a request," the reader says. "Never die too soon."

"Too soon? Look at me. I'm the duck hanging too long on its hook in the window—past eating. The only difference?"

"Yes," the reader says. "What is the difference between you and the duck on the hook?"

"The duck," Author says, "at least knows when it's time to be dead."

The old man stares at Author, considering.

"My father," he says, "hung himself at ninety-seven years old. He couldn't take it any longer. That's what he said in his note. He didn't want to face living anymore."

"I'm sorry to hear that."

"I wish he'd spoken to me," the old man says. "I'd have

told him. Ninety-seven? No need for such drastic action, Father. Patience. Just give it a little time."

. . .

Forgive the author his relentless commitment. Forgive him his belief that even if the next city promises nothing more than this one old man, still it's his obligation to drive on. A writer never knows if perseverance is his terrible weakness or his greatest strength. And with all those headlights floating divided in his rearview mirror, Author never can tell which belong to his reader, which pair is his beacon, a North Star, split, cast back, guiding him on.

The two arrive at a Denver bookstore, which is now half marijuana dispensary. A scheme, the owner says while dusting a beloved volume, to use one drug to pay for another. After an empty-but-for-his-lone-reader reading, it's this man, flush with cash and good living, who tells Author to take any book he wants for his troubles. A gift of the store.

"Babel," Author says, surprising himself. "The early stories." He'd not let himself read them since he was a boy.

From Denver, Author crosses the Rockies toward the Pacific, with his reader (ever mindful of the speed limit) in hot pursuit. At Salt Lake City, Author hangs a northerly right and drives up to Vancouver through three days of rain. After reading for his reader in that lush city, Author turns his car toward the next bookstore, making his way back down the West Coast. The sun is with him this time, and Author drives with an arm stuck out the window, cooking his left side to a burn. At a gas station just north of Seattle, Author fills his tank with the last of the money he has. He is so strapped for cash that, a few miles farther on, he stops at a church-run stand by the side of the road. There, he sells the Babel he's only just been given for a dollar and watches the lady drop it into a box after marking it for two. "The stories," he tells her, "are just the way I remember."

Pulling into Seattle, a city where Author was once truly renowned, he knows, literally and figuratively, how low he's been laid. That his old friend, the buyer for Elliott Bay Books, has arranged to host Author for a reading is an act of charity so undisguised, it leaves him humbled enough to receive another. Eyes down, Author enters the Come Unto Me Mission across the street from the bookshop and eats a bowl of soup, his first meal of the day.

Inside the bookshop, Author gives his name to the pierced-nosed clerk behind the counter. She tells him, without any emotion, that his reading is downstairs. Author is crestfallen as he approaches the basement steps. Then he hears the noise, and his heart is set aflutter at the sound of a reception in full swing. The energy, he can feel it in his feet through the floorboards. Author stops himself from taking the stairs two at a time.

There is indeed a crowd assembled when he reaches the basement. They are coffee drinkers filling a bookstore café. Author asks the barista, and she points. The reading is in a tiny room beyond.

How the noise had confused Author, how it had filled him with glee.

When the book buyer shows up, he finds Author waiting in the little room, and the years wash away. All that time nothing but a blink when there's warmth between two people. They hug, and the buyer says, "You look good, just the same."

Before the emptiness of the room sours the moment, the buyer tackles it head-on. "I'm really sorry," he says. "It's a great book. This, the no-show, it's not you, it's us. It's been slow this season. Numbers are down."

"It's all right," Author says. "The whole country is, for me, a desert—empty rooms from sea to shining sea." It feels so good to tell it to this man who knew how it once was, who'd orchestrated Author's glorious sellout night a dozen years before, and yet who—with grace—now has acknowledged what *is*. Not like his reader. Not like his shadow, drowning him in faith. Author says, "You know what? Let's not even wait. How about, for old time's sake, let's just get a drink—you and me?"

The buyer considers and then throws an arm over Author's shoulder. "Sure, I'd love that," he says. He drops his arm and slides through the café toward the stairs with the author, wistful, behind.

As they climb, Author hears it. He is surprised he does, with the music and the chatter, but there it is, from deep in the mix of the café. "Author! Writer! It's time to start" is what he hears. "Writer, hello, where do you go?"

The book buyer half hears it himself—enough to pause, banister in hand. Author won't have it. He keeps climbing, driving the buyer on. And Author's old man—too slow to catch up and all those stairs before him—screams from below with all he's got. "Hey, writer!" he calls, and then, "Hey, bookstore man! A customer down here! The writer must read!"

This, the book buyer doesn't miss. "Would you listen to that?" he says. "Your public calling." Before he says more, the author, hangdog, turns and heads downstairs.

. . .

The reading is starting, but no one from the café comes in. Conversations continue. The music blares. It takes no small effort on the part of the buyer to convince the barista to turn the sound system down. There is—Author hears it—a low round of boos.

The old man sits in the front row in the tiny three-row back room. Small as it is, there's still a plywood stage, a foot high and not much deeper, with a little lectern perched at an angle, from which the author will read.

The emotion on Author's face is clear. And the buyer waits for him to compose himself, though it's quickly becoming obvious that Author's despair is anything but subsiding. It seems to be frothing into a rage aimed, inexplicably, at the frail little man.

"Buddy," the buyer says, trying to steer Author to the stage, "how about you just give the guy five minutes and then we'll grab us that drink?" The buyer, without even noticing, is kneading Author's shoulders and patting his back, as if coaxing him into the ring.

"Yes, five minutes," the old man says. "Now up! Up on that stage. Time to start."

This sets the author off.

"Stalker!" Author screams.

"Patron!"

"Do you understand how crazy it is?" Author says.

"Do you understand how crazy it is—*you*?"

Author stands silent, visibly shaking. The old man turns to the buyer, assuming he's taken the author's side.

"Tell me, why is the artist a romantic for surviving on a glimmer of hope? Why not the same for the reader? Why is my commitment a weaker thing? I came," the old man says, "he reads!"

The author, as if the two men are alone in the world, screams back. "I won't. Devil! Devilish, devilish old man."

The old man is laughing. To the buyer, he says, "He'll read, you'll see." And to Author, adamant, demanding: "Tell this bookman so he understands. Tell him what's really at stake in your heart and mine."

Author does not want to cry. He can feel his eyes wet, and goes as far as tipping his head back, praying a tear won't fall.

"What? What?" the old man says, a hand cupped to his ear.

Author says, "It will not, aloud, sound so good."

"Tell him!" the old man yells, pointing to the buyer. "Tell him why a man like you does what he does."

"I write," Author says, his face twisted into a wince, "to touch people in the way that I, as a reader, have been touched." And here his expression unwinds. "And if I were still any good at all, it wouldn't be just you two here listening. A failure, I admit it. Now you," he says to the old man, "admit it, too."

"Self-pity. The lament of the aging beauty queen. No," the reader says, "I won't admit failure for a book written for the ages."

The two men stand there facing each other, Author now openly weeping. They are caught in a moment so large and so raw that they do not notice that the cell-phone ringers have gone silent and the coffee machine has lost its terrible hiss, that the chatter is missing from the next room as the whole of that coffee shop, drawn by the screaming, now crowds around the doorway, watching their fight.

It's the woman from behind the counter, pierced and tatted and hair streaked blue. "Come on, read," she says, her call immediately backed up by another. "Get up there," someone yells. And another screams, "Hey, one old guy, give the other old guy his due." A sizable audience is forming. Gunged up with all his blubbering and sniffling, Author takes his book and a stiff-kneed step up to the stage. He will read tonight to a mob.

"Oh, no!" the old man yells. "Not this way." He gets behind the door and, with feet dug in, he pushes hard against it, attempting to close it on the assembled hipsters, who do not immediately retreat. "Out!" he yells. "Out, out, stylish young people!"

The old man frees a hand and points at Author onstage, so

that only the pointing hand is visible to those on the café side of the door. "This man, a legend! Not a trained cat from a Russian circus," he yells. "You listen for the right reasons. This is not a monkey who will ride a dog for a show." And when the old man says, "Russian," Author, watching from the stage, thinks, "Russian," and remembers the story of a promised dovecot. He sees a pair of Babel's bloody birds broken at his feet.

The old man keeps on with his pushing until the door is shut. During the scuffle, his black, black hair has somehow flipped in the wrong direction, his part reversed. That miraculous hair, which Author was sure was left untouched by time, reveals itself to be a separate color underneath. It is the sick yellow of straw. Author's reader for once looks his properly petrified age. And the reader, somehow sensing this, hurriedly flips his hair back to where it belongs. His hand, so much worse than Author's, spills over with tremors.

"Me and him," the old man says to Author while pulling the bookseller toward him. "Why not read for this nice pair, who both know and understand?"

Author opens his novel to a random page—symbolic. He gets ready to read from memory, to recite for his relentless pursuer. He will read the old man's favorite part. Author starts in, unintelligible, with the echoes of all his hemming and crying and a rattle to his voice.

He has not read two lines when he stops. He puts a hand up to signal that he's only pausing, and Author pulls from his back pocket a small, soft notebook, its spiral gone. It is where Author, secretly, involuntarily, and against better judgment, makes his endless notes. It is where he sketches a new book, for which no one will wait, and of which no one will hear. Pulling the rubber band off, he knows his reader won't live to see it, even if Author soldiers on to see it done.

"Something new I've been working on," Author says. And

the old man nods, full of respect. And the bookseller, who has been standing until now, nods as well, taking a seat at the reader's side.

And Author, who has played bigger and larger, who has, under all the pressure in the world, executed such evenings with aplomb, wipes his nose on his sleeve, takes a deep breath, and—leaning down close to the little book—reads on with all he's got.

Author reads for Seattle; it has always been his city. He reads for the buyer, who has always believed. Author reads one more time to his old man. He smiles at his reader, and reads on through the tears. Author reads on. And Author reads on.

Free Fruit
for Young Widows

W hen the Egyptian president Gamal Abdel Nasser took control of the Suez Canal, threatening Western access to that vital route, an agitated France shifted allegiances, joining forces with Britain and Israel against Egypt. This is a fact neither here nor there, except that during the 1956 Sinai Campaign there were soldiers in the Israeli army and soldiers in the Egyptian army who ended up wearing identical French-supplied uniforms to battle.

Not long into the fighting, an Israeli platoon came to rest at a captured Egyptian camp to the east of Bir Gafgafa, in the Sinai Desert. There Private Shimmy Gezer (formerly Shimon Bibberblat, of Warsaw, Poland) sat down to eat at a makeshift outdoor mess. Four armed commandos sat down with him. He grunted. They grunted. Shimmy dug into his lunch.

A squad mate of Shimmy came over to join them. Professor Tendler (who was then only Private Tendler, not yet a professor, and not yet even in possession of a high school degree) placed the tin cup that he was carrying on the edge of the table, taking care not to spill his tea. Then he took up his gun and shot each of the commandos in the head.

They fell quite neatly. The first two, who had been facing Professor Tendler, tipped back off the bench into the sand. The second pair, who had their backs to the Professor and were still staring openmouthed at their dead friends, fell facedown, the sound of their skulls hitting the table somehow more violent than the report of the gun.

Shocked by the murder of four fellow soldiers, Shimmy Gezer tackled his friend. To Professor Tendler, who was much bigger than Shimmy, the attack was more startling than threatening. Tendler grabbed hold of Shimmy's hands while screaming, "Egyptians! Egyptians!" in Hebrew. He was using the same word about the same people in the same desert that had been used thousands of years before. The main difference, if the old stories are to be believed, was that God no longer raised His own fist in the fight.

Professor Tendler quickly managed to contain Shimmy in a bear hug. "Egyptian commandos—confused," Tendler said, switching to Yiddish. "The enemy. The enemy joined you for lunch."

Shimmy listened. Shimmy calmed down.

Professor Tendler, thinking the matter was settled, let Shimmy go. As soon as he did, Shimmy swung wildly. He continued attacking, because who cared who those four men were? They were people. They were human beings who had sat down at the wrong table for lunch. They were dead people who had not had to die.

"You could have taken them prisoner!" Shimmy yelled. "Halt!" he screamed in German. "That's all—Halt!" Then, with tears streaming and fists flying, Shimmy said, "You didn't have to shoot."

By then, Professor Tendler had had enough. He proceeded to beat Shimmy Gezer. He didn't just defend himself. He didn't subdue his friend. He flipped Shimmy over, straddled his body, and pounded it down until it was level with the sand. He beat his friend until his friend couldn't take any more beating, and then he beat him some more. Finally, he climbed off Shimmy, looked up into the hot sun, and pushed through the crowd of soldiers who had assembled in the minutes since the Egyptians sat down to their fate. Tendler went off to have a smoke.

For those who had come running at the sound of gunfire and found five bodies in the sand, it was the consensus that a pummeled Shimmy Gezer looked to be in the worst condition of the bunch.

. . .

At the fruit-and-vegetable stand that Shimmy Gezer eventually opened in Jerusalem's Mahane Yehuda Market, his son, little Etgar, asked about the story of Professor Tendler again and again. From the time he was six, Etgar had worked the *duchan* at his father's side whenever he wasn't in school. At that age, knowing only a child's version of the story—that Tendler had done something in one of the wars that upset Etgar's father, and Etgar's father had jumped on the man, and the man had (his father never hesitated to admit) beat him up very badly— Etgar couldn't understand why his father was so nice to the Professor now. Reared, as he was, on the laws of the small family business, Etgar couldn't grasp why he was forbidden to accept a single lira from Tendler. The Professor got his vegetables free.

After Etgar weighed the tomatoes and the cucumbers, his father would take up the bag, stick in a nice fat eggplant, unasked, and pass it over to Professor Tendler.

"Kach," his father would say. "Take it. And wish your wife well."

. . .

As Etgar turned nine and ten and eleven, the story began to fill out. He was told about the commandos and the uniforms, about shipping routes and the Suez, and the Americans and the British and the French. He learned about the shots to the head. He learned about all the wars his father had fought in—'73, '67, '56, '48—though Shimmy Gezer still stopped short of the one he'd first been swept up in, the war that ran from 1939 to 1945.

Etgar's father explained the hazy morality of combat, the split-second decisions, the assessment of threat and response, the nature of percentages and absolutes. Shimmy did his best to make clear to his son that Israelis—in their nation of unfinished borders and unwritten constitution—were trapped in a gray space that was called real life.

In this gray space, he explained, even absolutes could maintain more than one position, reflect more than one truth. "You, too," he said to his son, "may someday face a decision such as Professor Tendler's—may you never know from it." He pointed at the bloody stall across from theirs, pointed at a fish below the mallet, flopping on the block. "God forbid you should have to live with the consequences of decisions, permanent, eternal, that will chase you in your head, turning from this side to that, tossing between wrong and right."

But Etgar still couldn't comprehend how his father saw the story to be that of a fish flip-flopping, when it was, in his eyes, only ever about that mallet coming down.

. . .

Etgar wasn't one for the gray. He was a tiny, thoughtful, bucktoothed boy of certainties. And, every Friday when Tendler came by the stand, Etgar would pack up the man's produce and then run through the story again, searching for black and white.

This man had saved his father's life, but maybe he hadn't. He'd done what was necessary, but maybe he could have done it another way. And even if the basic school-yard rule applied in adult life—that a beating delivered earns a beating in return—did it ever justify one as fierce as the beating his father had described? A pummeling so severe that Shimmy, while telling the story, would run Etgar's fingers along his left cheek to show him where Professor Tendler had flattened the bone.

Even if the violence had been justified, even if his father didn't always say, "You must risk your friend's life, your family's, your own, you must be willing to die—even to save the life of your enemy—if ever, of two deeds, the humane one may be done," it was not his father's act of forgiveness, but his kindness that baffled Etgar.

Shimmy would send him running across Agrippas Street to bring back two cups of coffee or two glasses of tea to welcome Professor Tendler, telling Etgar to snatch a good-size handful of pistachios from Eizenberg's cart along the way. This treatment his father reserved only for his oldest friends.

And absolutely no one but the war widows got their produce free. Quietly and with dignity, so as to cause these women no shame, Etgar's father would send them off with fresh fruit and big bags of vegetables, sometimes for years after their losses. He always took care of the young widows. When they protested, he'd say, "You sacrifice, I sacrifice. All in all, what's a bag of apples?"

"It's all for one country," he'd say.

When it came to Professor Tendler, so clear an answer never came.

. . .

When Etgar was twelve, his father acknowledged the complexities of Tendler's tale.

"Do you want to know why I can care for a man who once

beat me? Because to a story, there is context. There is always context in life."

"That's it?" Etgar asked.

"That's it."

.   .   .

At thirteen, he was told a different story. Because at thirteen, Etgar was a man.

"You know I was in the war," Shimmy said to his son. The way he said it, Etgar knew that he didn't mean '48 or '56, '67 or '73. He did not mean the Jewish wars, in all of which he had fought. He meant the big one. The war that no one in his family but Shimmy had survived, which was also the case for Etgar's mother. This was why they had taken a new name, Shimmy explained. In the whole world, the Gezers were three.

"Yes," Etgar said. "I know."

"Professor Tendler was also in that war," Shimmy said.

"Yes," Etgar said.

"It was hard on him," Shimmy said. "And that is why, why I am always nice."

Etgar thought. Etgar spoke.

"But you were there, too. You've had the same life as him. And you'd never have shot four men, even the enemy, if you could have taken them prisoner, if you could have spared a life. Even if you were in danger, you'd risk—" Etgar's father smiled, and stopped him.

"*Kodem kol,*" he said, "a similar life is not a same life. There is a difference." Here Shimmy's face turned serious, the lightness gone. "In that first war, in that big war, I was the lucky one," he said. "In the Shoah, I survived."

"But he's here," Etgar said. "He survived, just the same as you."

"No," Etgar's father said. "He made it through the camps. He walks, he breathes, and he was very close to making it out of Europe alive. But they killed him. After the war, we still lost people. They killed what was left of him in the end."

For the first time, without Professor Tendler there, without one of Shimmy's friends from the ghetto who stopped by to talk in Yiddish, without one of the soldier buddies from his unit in the reserves or one of the kibbutzniks from whom he bought his fruits and his vegetables, Etgar's father sent Etgar across Agrippas Street to get two glasses of tea. One for Etgar and one for him.

"Hurry," Shimmy said, sending Etgar off with a slap on his behind. Before Etgar had taken a step, his father grabbed his collar and popped open the register, handing him a brand-new ten-shekel bill. "And buy us a nice big bag of seeds from Eizenberg. Tell him to keep the change. You and I, we are going to sit awhile."

Shimmy took out the second folding chair from behind the register. It would also be the first time that father and son had ever sat down in the store together. Another rule of good business: A customer should always find you standing. Always there's something you can be doing—sweeping, stacking, polishing apples. The customers will come to a place where there is pride.

·   ·   ·

This is why Professor Tendler got his tomatoes free, why the sight of the man who beat Shimmy made his gaze go soft with kindness in the way that it did when one of the *miskenot* came by—why it took on what Etgar called his father's Free-Fruit-for-Young-Widows eyes. This is the story that Shimmy told Etgar when he felt that his boy was a man:

The first thing Professor Tendler saw when his death camp was liberated were two big, tough American soldiers fainting dead away. The pair (presumably war-hardened) stood before the immense, heretofore unimaginable brutality of modern extermination, frozen, slack-jawed before a mountain of putrid, naked corpses, a hill of men.

And from this pile of broken bodies that had been—prior to the American invasion—set to be burned, a rickety, skeletal Tendler stared back. Professor Tendler stared and studied, and when he was sure that those soldiers were not Nazi soldiers, he crawled out from his hiding place among the corpses, pushing and shoving those balsa-wood arms and legs aside.

It was this hill of bodies that had protected Tendler day after day. The poor Sonderkommando who dumped the bodies, as well as those who came to cart them to the ovens, knew that the boy was inside. They brought him the crumbs of their crumbs to keep him going. And though it was certain death for these prisoners to protect him, it allowed them a sliver of humanity in their inhuman jobs. This was what Shimmy was trying to explain to his son—that these palest shadows of kindness were enough to keep a dead man alive.

When Tendler finally got to his feet, straightening his body out, when the corpse that was Professor Tendler at age thirteen—"your age"—came crawling from that nightmare, he looked at the two Yankee soldiers, who looked at him and then hit the ground with a thud.

Professor Tendler had already seen so much in life that this was not worth even a pause, and so he walked on. He walked on naked through the gates of the camp, walked on until he got some food and some clothes, walked on until he had shoes and then a coat. He walked on until he had a little bread and a potato in his pocket—a surplus.

Soon there was also in that pocket a cigarette and then a second, a coin and then a second. Surviving in this way, Tendler walked across borders until he was able to stand straight and tall, until he showed up in his childhood town in a matching suit of clothes, with a few bills in his pocket and, in his waistband, a six-shooter with five bullets chambered, in order to protect himself during the nights that he slept by the side of the road.

Professor Tendler was expecting no surprises, no reunions. He'd seen his mother killed in front of him, his father, his three sisters, his grandparents, and, after some months in the camp, the two boys he knew from back home.

But home—that was the thing he held on to. Maybe his house was still there, and his bed. Maybe the cow was still giving milk, and the goats still chewing garbage, and his dog still barking at the chickens as before. And maybe his other family—the nurse at whose breast he had become strong (before weakened), her husband, who had farmed his father's field, and their son (his age), and another (two years younger), boys with whom he had played like a brother—maybe this family was still there waiting. Waiting for him to come home.

Tendler could make a new family in that house. He could call every child he might one day have by his dead loved ones' names.

The town looked as it had when he'd left. The streets were his streets, the linden trees in the square taller but laid out as before. And when Tendler turned down the dirt road that led to his gate, he fought to keep himself from running, and he fought to keep himself from crying, because, after what he had seen, he knew that to survive in this world he must always act like a man.

So Tendler buttoned his coat and walked quietly toward

the fence, wishing that he had a hat to take off as he passed through the gate—just the way the man of the house would when coming home to what was his.

But when he saw her in the yard—when he saw Fanushka, his nurse, their maid—the tears came anyway. Tendler popped a precious button from his coat as he ran to her and threw himself into her arms, and he cried for the first time since the trains.

With her husband at her side, Fanushka said to him, "Welcome home, son," and "Welcome home, child," and "We prayed," "We lit candles," "We dreamed of your return."

When they asked, "Are your parents also coming? Are your sisters and your grandparents far behind?" and when they asked after all the old neighbors, house by house, Tendler answered, not by metaphor, and not by insinuation. When he knew the fate, he stated it as it was: beaten or starved, shot, cut in half, the front of the head caved in. All this he related without feeling—matters, each, of fact. All this he shared before venturing a step through his front door.

Looking through that open door, Tendler decided that he would live with these people as family until he had a family of his own. He would grow old in this house. Free to be free, he would gate himself up again. But it would be his gate, his lock, his world.

A hand on his hand pulled him from his reverie. It was Fanushka talking, a sad smile on her face. "Time to fatten you up," she said. "A feast for first dinner." And she grabbed the chicken at her feet and twisted its neck right there in the yard. "Come in," she said while the animal twitched. "The master of the house has returned."

"Just as you left it," she said. "Only a few of our things."

Tendler stepped inside.

It was exactly as he remembered it—the table, the chairs—except that all that was personal was gone.

Fanushka's two sons came in, and Tendler understood what time had done. These boys, fed and housed, warmed and loved, were fully twice his size. He felt, then, something he had never known in the camps, a civilized emotion that would have served no use. Tendler felt ashamed. He turned red, clenched his jaw tight, and felt his gums bleeding into his mouth.

"You have to understand," Etgar's father said to his son. "These boys, his brothers, they were now twice his size and strangers to him."

The boys, prodded, shook hands with Tendler. They did not know him anymore.

.　.　.

"Still, it is a nice story," Etgar said. "Sad. But also happy. He makes it home to a home. It's what you always say. Survival, that's what matters. Surviving to start again."

Etgar's father held up a sunflower seed, thinking about this. He cracked it between his front teeth.

"So they are all making a dinner for Professor Tendler," he said. "And he is sitting on the kitchen floor, legs crossed, as he did when he was a boy, and he is watching. Watching happily, drinking a glass of goat's milk, still warm. And then the father goes out to slaughter that goat. 'A feast for dinner,' he says. 'A chicken's not enough.' Professor Tendler, who has not had meat in years, looks at him, and the father, running a nail along his knife, says, 'I remember the kosher way.'"

Tendler was so happy that he could not bear it. So happy and so sad. And, with the cup of warm milk and the warm feeling, Tendler had to pee. But he didn't want to move now that he was there with his other mother and, resting on her shoulder, a baby sister. A year and a half old and one curl on the head. A little girl, fat and happy. Fat in the ankle, fat in the wrist.

Professor Tendler rushed out at the last second, out of the warm kitchen, out from under his roof. Professor Tendler, a man whom other men had tried to turn into an animal, did not race to the outhouse. It didn't cross his mind. He stood right under the kitchen window to smell the kitchen smells, to stay close. And he took a piss. Over the sound of the stream, he heard his nurse lamenting.

He knew what she must be lamenting—the Tendler family destroyed.

He listened to what she was saying. And he heard.

"He will take everything" is what she said. "He will take it all from us—our house, our field. He'll snatch away all we've built and protected, everything that has been—for so long—ours."

There outside the window, pissing and listening, and also "disassociating," as Professor Tendler would call it (though he did not then have the word), he knew only that he was watching himself from above, that he could see himself feeling all the disappointment as he felt it, until he was keenly and wildly aware that he had felt nothing all those years, felt nothing when his father and mother were shot, felt nothing while in the camps, nothing, in fact, from the moment he was driven from his home to the moment he returned.

In that instant, Tendler's guilt was sharper than any sensation he had ever known.

And here, in response to his precocious son, Shimmy said, "Yes, yes, of course it was about survival—Tendler's way of coping. Of course he'd been feeling all along." But Tendler—a boy who had stepped over his mother's body and kept walking—had, for those peasants, opened up.

It was right then, Professor Tendler later told Shimmy, that he became a philosopher.

"He will steal it all away," Fanushka said. "Everything. He has come for our lives."

And her son, whom Tendler had considered a brother, said, "No." And Tendler's other almost brother said, "No."

"We will eat," Fanushka said. "We will celebrate. And when he sleeps, we will kill him." To one of the sons, she said, "Go. Tell your father to keep that knife sharp." To the other, she said, "You get to sleep early, and you get up early, and before you grab the first tit on that cow, I want his throat slit. Ours. Ours, not to be taken away."

Tendler ran. Not toward the street, but back toward the outhouse in time to turn around as the kitchen door flew open, in time to smile at the younger brother on his way to find his father, in time for Tendler to be heading back the right way.

"Do you want to hear what was shared at such a dinner?" Shimmy asked his son. "The memories roused and oaths sworn? There was wine, I know. 'Drink, drink,' the mother said. There was the chicken and a pot of goat stew. And, in a time of great deprivation, there was also sugar for the tea." At this, Shimmy pointed at the bounty of their stand. "And, as if nothing, next to the baby's basket on the kitchen floor sat a basket of apples. Tendler hadn't had an apple in who knows how long."

Tendler brought the basket to the table. The family laughed as he peeled the apples with a knife, first eating the peels, then the flesh, and savoring even the seeds and the cores. It was a celebration, a joyous night. So much so that Professor Tendler could not by its end, belly distended, eyes crossed with drink, believe what he knew to have been said.

There were hugs and there were kisses, and Tendler—the master of the house—was given his parents' bedroom upstairs, the two boys across the hall, and below, in the kitchen ("It will be warmest"), slept the mother and the father and the fat-ankled girl.

"Sleep well," Fanushka said. "Welcome home, my son." And, sweetly, she kissed Tendler on both eyes.

Tendler climbed the stairs. He took off his suit and went to bed. And that was where he was when Fanushka popped through the door and asked him if he was warm enough, if he needed a lamp by which to read.

"No, thank you," he said.

"So formal? No thanks necessary," Fanushka said. "Only 'Yes, Mother,' or 'No, Mother,' my poor reclaimed orphan son."

"No light, Mother," Tendler said, and Fanushka closed the door.

Tendler got out of bed. He put on his suit. Once again without any shame to his actions, Tendler searched the room for anything of value, robbing his own home.

Then he waited. He waited until the house had settled into itself, the last creak slipping from the floorboards as the walls pushed back against the wind. He waited until his mother, his Fanushka, must surely sleep, until a brother intent on staying up for the night—a brother who had never once fought for his life—convinced himself that it would be all right to close his eyes.

Tendler waited until he, too, had to sleep, and that's when he tied the laces of his shoes together and hung them over his shoulder. That's when he took his pillow with one hand and, with the other, quietly cocked his gun.

Then, with goose feathers flying, Tendler moved through the house. A bullet for each brother, one for the father and one for the mother. Tendler fired until he found himself standing in the warmth of the kitchen, one bullet left to protect him on the nights when he would sleep by the side of the road.

That last bullet Tendler left in the fat baby girl, because he did not know from mercy, and did not need to leave another of that family to grow to kill him at some future time.

. . .

"He murdered them," Etgar said. "A murderer."

"No," his father told him. "There was no such notion at the time."

"Even so, it is murder," Etgar said.

"If it is, then it's only fair. They killed him first. It was his right."

"But you always say—"

"Context."

"But the baby. The girl."

"The baby is hardest, I admit. But these are questions for the philosopher. These are the theoretical instances put into flesh and blood."

"But it's not a question. These people, they are not the ones who murdered his family."

"They were coming for him that night."

"He could have escaped. He could have run for the gate when he overheard. He didn't need to race back toward the outhouse, race to face the brother as he came the other way."

"Maybe there was no more running in him. Anyway, do you understand 'an eye for an eye'? Can you imagine a broader meaning of *self-defense*?"

"You always forgive him," Etgar said. "You suffered the same things—but you aren't that way. You would not have done what he did."

"It is hard to know what a person would and wouldn't do in any specific instance. And you, spoiled child, apply the rules of civilization to a boy who had seen only its opposite. Maybe the fault for those deaths lies in a system designed for the killing of Tendlers that failed to do its job. An error, a slip that allowed a Tendler, no longer fit, back loose in the world."

"Is that what you think?"

"It's what I ask. And I ask you, my Etgar, what you would have done if you were Tendler that night?"

"Not kill."

"Then you die."

"Only the grown-ups."

"But it was a boy who was sent to cut Tendler's throat."

"How about killing only those who would do harm?"

"Still it's murder. Still it is killing people who have yet to act, murdering them in their sleep."

"I guess," Etgar said. "I can see how they deserved it, the four. How I might, if I were him, have killed them."

Shimmy shook his head, looking sad.

"And whoever are we, my son, to decide who should die?"

. . .

It was on that day that Etgar Gezer became a philosopher himself. Not in the manner of Professor Tendler, who taught theories up at the university on the mountain, but, like his father, practical and concrete. Etgar would not finish high school or go to college, and, except for his three years in the army, he would spend his life—happily—working the stand in the *shuk*. He'd stack the fruit into pyramids and contemplate weighty questions with a seriousness of thought. And when there were answers, Etgar would try employing them to make for himself and others, in whatever small way, a better life.

It was on that day, too, that Etgar decided Professor Tendler was both a murderer and, at the same time, a *misken*. He believed he understood how and why Professor Tendler had come to kill that peasant family, and how men sent to battle in uniform—even in the same uniform—would find no mercy at his hand. Etgar also came to see how Tendler's story could just as easily have ended for the Professor that first night, back in his parents' room, in his parents' bed, a gun with four bullets held in a suicide's hand—how the first bullet Tendler ever fired might have been into his own head.

Still, every Friday, Etgar packed up Tendler's fruit and vegetables. And in that bag Etgar would add, when he had them, a pineapple or a few fat mangoes dripping honey. Handing it to Tendler, Etgar would say, "*Kach,* Professor. Take it." This, even after his father had died.

Acknowledgments

With deepest gratitude, I'd like to thank my truly-limitless-in-her-faith-and-inexhaustible-in-her-patience agent, Nicole Aragi, and the trusty Robin to her Batman, one Ms. Christie Hauser. Equally abundant thanks go to my amazing editor, Jordan Pavlin, who came to my first-ever reading and has offered a golden ear ever since. I'm much obliged to editorial assistant Leslie Levine, as well as all the fine folk at Knopf, especially Barbara de Wilde (who has designed all three covers) and Sara Eagle (spelled like the bird, as her voice mail attests). A huge thanks to Merle Englander, who read these stories forward and back, and who can spot a missing comma at a thousand yards. The same with Rachel Silver, who has the book's dedication, but belongs here, too. To my personal physician, Daniel Brodie; and to my first reader (and second opinion), Chris Adrian—a debt of gratitude is owed. And likewise to a truly generous soul, and my hairiest muse, Etgar Keret, who inspired not one story in this book but two. Finally, if you leave Etgar's apartment in Tel Aviv, head over to the central bus station, and take the #405 up the mountain to Jerusalem, you'll reach the man farthest away that I'd like to acknowledge, and that is Joel Weiss, who, when it comes to facts Hebraic, puts Google to shame.

blog and newsletter

For literary discussion, author insight,
book news, exclusive content,
recipes and giveaways, visit the
Weidenfeld & Nicolson blog and
sign up for the newsletter at:

www.wnblog.co.uk

For breaking news, reviews and exclusive competitions
Follow us 🐦 @wnbooks
Find us 📘 facebook.com/WeidenfeldandNicolson